Storm
at the
Edge of Time

Storm

at the

Edge of Time

Pamela F. Service

WALKER AND COMPANY

NEW YORK

First published in the United States of America in 1994 by Walker
Publishing Company, Inc.

Published simultaneously in Canada by Thomas Allen & Son Canada,
Limited, Markham, Ontario

Library of Congress Cataloging-in-Publication Data
Service, Pamela F.
Storm at the edge of time / Pamela F. Service.
p.   cm.
ISBN 0-8027-8306-6
I. Title.
PS3569.E737S76   1994
813'.54—dc20   93-50816
CIP

Book design by Claire Naylon Vaccaro

Printed in the United States of America

2   4   6   8   10   9   7   5   3   1

For Cousin Grace,
to recall her early years in Scotland.

Storm
at the
Edge of Time

WAITING

H e was waiting, but not patiently. He had never
been a patient man. Not when he was alive. And
not now.

Yet here he was, waiting. Eternally waiting while
the stones circled in dark silence around him.

At long last, though, the waiting was coming to an
end. The storm was about to break, the storm he had
been wrenched from the world to guard against. Yet
now he was powerless to stop it—almost powerless. The
tools he needed were out there, but it would take perfect timing and a long search to find them. A long, patient search.

Angrily the blue eyes glinted from the shadow of the
stones. He was not a patient man.

Chapter One

Under the steady urging of the wind, the sea crashed in billowing surges on the rocks below. The water was gray, a dark slaty gray laced with ridges of wind-whipped foam and churned to spray where the waves met the island's dark rocks. There would be no fishing boats out today, nor any longboats setting out on Viking raids. They would wait until spring, as they did every year in these northern isles.

Above him, the cold sky was a pale cloud-blanketed gray, stitched through by the occasional diving, crying seabird. But the boy had eyes only for the sea. Its crashing boom filled his ears and shook his body as he tried to weave into it a sound of his own, a harsh musical sound. It trembled about him, part song, part cry, part mystery, as he tried to weave it into the waves, to sink it into their depths.

"Arni Arnorson!" a voice jeered from behind him. "Might as well drop that last name of yours. Not only will a runt like you never make a warrior, you'll never even become a skald like your father—not with a voice like that."

Nervously shoving red hair from his eyes, Arni turned to face his familiar tormentor. A few feet away, Sven Havardson stood on a grassy hilltop with his usual companions just behind him.

"I don't want to be a skald!" Arni said, sounding more bold than he felt. "Singing the histories and sagas is all very fine, and my father's the best skald there is, but I am practicing to be something more."

"It sounded like you were practicing to be sick," Sven said, and the others broke into snickering laughter.

An angry flush spread over Arni's pale face. "I'm practicing to be a power-worker, a sorcerer. I was trying out a call for seals. My great-grandmother, Eithne the Sorceress, could call seals to her and talk with them."

"Not even a seal would want to talk with you," Sven said with a sneer, "but this is hardly the right season to look for seals."

Arni shrugged. "I know that, but I was just practicing. I want to get it right before any seals come and maybe misunderstand me."

The others laughed as the older boy stepped forward and scowled down at Arni. "Nobody misunderstands you, runt. We all know you're a weakling who's no good at anything and thinks he doesn't have to be because his father is the Earl's cousin and his skald. But suppose the priests hear about this new game of yours and decide you're one of those heretics who want to throw out the new church and return to the old ways?"

"You can't scare me," Arni lied. "Earl Thorfinn says Christianity shouldn't make us forget who we are."

Sven laughed and turned away. "You'll wish you *could* forget, if Brother Paul gives you a sermon on hellfire and damnation. Not even the Earl and his skald can save you from that." The boy swaggered off, gesturing to his companions. "Come on. Let's leave this failure to the seals."

Angrily, Arni turned back to the sea. The cold salt wind beat like needles against his flushed face. No, as proud as he was of his father, Arni wouldn't want his protection here. And he shouldn't need it! He shouldn't need protection from boring sermons or taunting bullies—or anything else either!

True, compared to the other boys he was as small and weak as a puppy. He'd never been much good at games or fishing or even swordplay, although he loved the feel of the sword and practiced with it every day. But he was sure he was good at something: magic. His great-grandmother had been a sorceress, after all, and his grandmother a healer. And his father was a skald, a famous one, who worked magic with words. So he was sure the power must be in him. He just had to get at it.

Arni sighed, staring down at the surf crashing against jaggedly layered rocks. Sven was right. Since the Earl's father had turned out the old Viking gods, Odin and Thor and all, in favor of this new Christian god, nobody would talk much about magic or help him find how to use the power he was so sure he had.

A sharp cry startled him. Arni looked toward it and saw a sleek black shape on a rock below. It turned its head. The day's pale light glinted in two large blue eyes. A seal!

For a moment, the two stared at each other; then, echoing the boy's earlier song, the seal dove into the gray water. Its dark form appeared and disappeared as it swam toward the main island.

Arni jumped up, excitedly watching, until the creature vanished from sight. Of course, probably he hadn't really called the thing. But still, he might have! And he wasn't going to let any priests or bullies tell him he couldn't.

He would find that power! And suddenly, watching the seal's course, he knew where to look—the stone circle over on the main island. It was old, older even than the Vikings and their gods. It had been on the island since the time when the people of Orkney had worshiped far different powers, powers of earth and air and deep magic. But the circle must have power still, or these new priests wouldn't warn people to stay away from it and from the other ancient stones. They were evil, the priests said.

But maybe, Arni thought, the stones were not evil. They might just have powers that the priests could not understand. But *he* would! Excitedly, Arni hurried off. When he decided to do something, he didn't like to wait a moment to get started.

And he wouldn't have to. It was morning still, and the tide was out so he could cross from their defensible tidal island to the main island on its east. The wind buffeted his hair and his yellow woolen cape as he trotted along the sheep path skirting the cliff's edge, his mind already fixed on his goal.

From the waves below, eyes watched him. Impatient blue eyes.

Tyaak sat on a rock, staring glumly over the bleak island landscape. Supposedly it was now summer on the northern part of this planet, but still a cold wind blew steadily from the surrounding blue-gray sea. On his home world, a rare wind that strong would shiver through the cycla trees, setting their leaves tinkling and flashing pink and gold in the warm sun. But here there weren't any trees, not even the green-leaved ones that grew on the rest of this planet. The only color here came from the blue sky, the pale green grass, and the low purple plants that splotched the empty hillsides.

Standing up, Tyaak ran a hand through his blue-black hair, trying to get it to stand up properly. But it was no use. None of this was any use. Sullenly he tromped down the hillside, crushing the spongy plants as he went. He had given up looking for paths. The few wild animals that lived here didn't make them, and most of the ancient roads had long since grown over. The natives that still lived on this island stayed mainly in the remains of the town, either as eccentric hermits or tending to the needs of the few tourists who came this way.

Well, he was no tourist, Tyaak thought bitterly. He didn't even want to be on this planet, let alone this island. But this was his Nri Irll initiation. The choice of place had not been his. And here he was, stuck with the bleak island his mother's stock had left centuries ago.

Still, his parents might have been less harsh. All that was required of a young Kreeth on the verge of adulthood was to go somewhere alone. Somewhere with no diversions, where a person could walk and think about life. Well, here he was, walking and thinking, but his thoughts were not uplifting ones.

All his life he had tried so hard to be Kreeth—to make his parents proud of him, to let them and all his doubting peers see how much he was like his Kreeth father instead of his Human mother. He had tried to have nothing to do with anything Human, and even his mother hadn't objected much. Why should she? After all, the Kreeth were so obviously superior to Humans. If that weren't so, why was it that the Kreeth dominated this portion of the Galactic Union, while the Humans simply drifted around it as explorers, artists, or farmers?

The Humans had even drifted away from their own planet—not that he could blame them. They had so polluted its waters, depleted its atmosphere, and wasted its resources that if the Kreeth had not found them some centuries back, they would probably be extinct by now. The history he'd been forced to read about this world had been a sorry one.

No loss, he thought bitterly, except that without Human stock he wouldn't have been born. But he needn't let being half Human defeat him! He was training to be a navigator like his father, not a musician like his mother. Admittedly, his skin was far too muddy a green and his hair too dark a blue. But his dress and manners were perfectly Kreeth—and his hairstyle would be, too, if only this infernal wind would stop blowing it about!

Angrily he raked fingers through his sagging hair,

then gave up, letting the dark mane bob and flutter limply about his head. His age-mates at least accepted his odd appearance, though they never let him forget his mixed heritage. He had hoped that once he was considered an adult, they would ignore that, too. But doing his Nri Irll on Earth, of all places, certainly wouldn't help.

At the base of the hillside, Tyaak looked about. Coarse green grass and low purple plants stretched in all directions, broken here and there by the gray heaps of abandoned ruins. Ahead, two arms of the sea—or maybe one was a lake—pinched the land into a narrow thread.

Really, there was no point in going farther in this direction, except that he had to go somewhere. Kreeth believed that the best time to think was while walking, and on his Nri Irll Tyaak wasn't supposed to return to his ship until night. Not that anyone was here to tell on him, but he wanted to be fully Kreeth, to do everything exactly right.

Scanning the landscape ahead, Tyaak looked for some goal. He always felt better when he had specific goals. A movement caught his attention. A Human? No, it had four feet. Some native animal, then. It was walking up a slight slope, just beyond where the waters nearly joined. The ground there was unmarked except for a few tall stones. Or were they some sort of branchless tree? More house ruins, maybe? No, these were different. He pulled out his distance scanner and raised it to his eyes. The image jumped into focus.

The animal was brownish and slender, with bony branches rising from its head. As if it sensed being watched, it raised its head and looked Tyaak's way. He could see its wide blue eyes, the same odd blue this planet's skies and seas had when not troubled by the frequent clouds.

Tyaak shifted his scanner to the objects beyond. Clearly they were stones, large irregular stones standing . upright. Moving the scanner, he saw that others lay half hidden in the vegetation. They seemed to form some sort of pattern—a circle, perhaps. Obviously they were not a natural outcrop, and not a ruined house, either.

Tyaak shrugged and replaced the scanner in his belt. Not that he cared what they were, but they were a goal, something to turn his bored footsteps toward. Meanwhile, his thoughts could stubbornly trudge over the same ground. Why had his parents chosen this has-been planet as a place to "learn about himself"? This barren rock represented all the things about himself he wanted to forget. A world reeking with Humans, with their barbaric ways, their primitive animal instincts. Tyaak shivered. He had nothing to do with that. Nothing! Doggedly he marched on.

In the distant heather, the deer stopped grazing. With keen blue eyes, it impatiently watched the boy's grudging advance.

The first child had been relatively easy, the watcher reflected. Belief is a simple thing to play upon. For the final one, the timing had been tricky, but ignorance is even easier to use than belief. But with the middle one, ignorance and belief were almost evenly mixed, raising stubborn walls of fear. That one would be a different story.

Chapter Two

Jamie was trying hard not to be disappointed. But this was very nearly the last straw.

She stepped out of the car and looked grimly at the house. It looked back just as grimly. Hopeless! Gray stone, like everything else on this cold bleak island. Big and solid, but hardly the "Scottish mansion" she had envisioned. No turrets, no interesting angles, no likelihood of secret rooms or mysterious abandoned wings. Even a cheap dollhouse would have had a more imaginative layout. "A typical Orkney house," her mother had gushed when they'd driven up. Two stories, central stairs, each floor with two rooms in front and two in back, a chimney at each windowless end. The whole boring box capped with a gray slate roof patched with lichen.

No mystery, no glamour, and definitely no inkling of ghosts!

"Jamie Halcro!" her father called. "Stop gawking and help me get the luggage out of the boot." He smiled, relishing the quaint English term.

"Trunk," Jamie muttered as she yanked her suitcase from the tumble of luggage. She staggered with it through the open gate in the stone wall and into the yard. Some yard: scruffy pale grass, with a few wind-shivering daffodils lining the path. Not even one tree. In fact, they hadn't seen any trees on Orkney since they'd left that little port town on the south coast. It was too windy and cold even for trees.

The thought of that port reminded her of the four-hour ferry trip from the north coast of Scotland. Over the sea to her father's generations-back ancestral home. Her stomach lurched. Seasick. She'd never known one little word could spell such misery. And definitely, this island had not been worth the suffering.

She stepped through the front door. The house smelled dank, with a sharp overtone of coal smoke. The house-rental lady had started a fire for them in the sitting room and was still puttering around. Jamie hauled her suitcase upstairs. It would take more than one measly fire to drive the cold and damp out of this place.

"Choose whichever room you want," her mother called cheerily from below. Jamie plunked her bag on the landing and opened a door. The room was dark, its one window looking up a hillside of pale grass and purple brown leather. Not much of a view. The other room in the back was a bathroom, with one of those stupid showers on timers that she'd struggled with on their trip up from London.

Both front rooms had a view over fields and a couple

of lochs to a gray stretch of open sea beyond. One room had blue bedspreads and a painting of fishing boats. She took it. It wasn't quite as blah as the pink-bedspread room with the painting of smug nesting ducks.

Heaving her suitcase on one bed, she flopped onto the other and stared up at the white-plastered ceiling. Face it, Jamie, she told herself, you really lost out this time. As usual, her can-do-no-wrong brother had come out on top. He was spending his college spring break with friends in Florida. But of course, a mere middle school student like her couldn't do that sort of thing. No, she had to be dragged along on another of her parents' birding vacations. Why couldn't they ever look at birds on warm tropical beaches with palm trees?

After her initial outrage, Jamie had been consoling herself with the thought of staying on a romantic island in a 300-year-old Scottish mansion. A place like that, she had figured, was sure to have ghosts. At long last, she would see ghosts.

Not that she hadn't tried before. She'd been trying since she'd first heard about ghosts, at age three on Halloween. But so far all of her Ouija boards, seances, and hanging out in graveyards hadn't produced one wisp of a ghost.

Still, she had psychic powers; she *knew* she did. Maybe she couldn't draw like her father the commercial artist; maybe she couldn't cope with numbers like her mother the accountant; and certainly she wasn't clever with juggling words, like her debate-team captain and would-be lawyer brother. But surely she must have *some* talent. Being sensitive to the supernatural, Jamie had decided long ago, was it.

She used to experiment with all kinds of things supernatural. But most of it had been creepy, stupid made-up stuff. Ghosts, though, were different. Throughout history responsible, grown-up people had believed in ghosts. And now she'd decided that this must be where her talent lay. Surely she could see ghosts.

Up to now, the problem must have been the setting. There just weren't any ghosts around when she'd tried to conjure them up. After all, America was a pretty new country, as history went, and Jamie lived in a very new house in a very new suburb. Not much time for lost souls to build up there. Even the local cemetery wasn't much help. Instead of having spooky tilted tombstones, the graves were marked with neat little plaques lying flat on the ground so as not to trouble the riding lawn mowers. What unquiet spirit would hang around a place like that?

But Scotland: That place was *old*. And Jamie'd read enough British kids' books to know that Scotland was teeming with old mansions, ruined abbeys, castles, and dungeons—and ancient graveyards where tombstones jutted through the weeds like hags' teeth.

So now here she was, and the place looked anything but promising. Still, there had to be ghosts somewhere around here. And she would find them! There was no way she was going to admit she had no talent for anything.

Laughing wryly, Jamie sat up. Her brother always teased her by claiming that she was at least stubborn enough to be a lawyer—stubborn and goal-oriented. Well, now she had a goal.

With renewed energy, she trotted back downstairs and got her overnight bag out of the car. The house-rental lady was just leaving. Jamie wavered a moment, then decided. If she was going to make a fool of herself, she might as well get started.

"Excuse me," Jamie said as the woman opened her car door. "This is really an old house. I suppose it must be haunted—at least a little bit?"

The woman looked shocked. "Haunted? No, no, don't you worry. I never heard of it being haunted, I assure you."

"No, really, it wouldn't bother us," Jamie said urgently. "I mean we'd still want to rent it and everything."

"Well, I am glad of that. But I am sure that everyone who lived in this house was too well behaved to leave any ghosts about." Smiling weakly, the woman climbed into her car and drove away.

Jamie just stared after the car. "Too well behaved?" she said to herself. "Bah! Too boring, more likely."

Her "bah" was echoed from across the road, where several sheep grazed on the coarse grass. One of them rubbed itself on a tall irregular stone standing in the pasture. From the gray sky, a seagull flashed down and landed on the stone. Looking at Jamie with sharp blue eyes, it let out a raucous laughing cry.

"Shut up, you stupid bird!" Jamie snapped as she tromped back inside. "The sheep has it right. 'Bah' on the whole thing." With an indignant-sounding squawk, the bird flew off over the fields.

That night they made dinner from cans of soup, spaghetti, and rice pudding they found in the cupboard.

Boring, but Jamie wasn't too interested in food. Her stomach was still reliving the ferry trip, and her head was still out of whack after the jet flight from the United States. She poked at her meal while her parents talked eagerly of the bird species they hoped to see.

"It's the right season for skuas and kittiwakes," her father said. "Did you know, Jamie, that there are over three hundred and thirty species of birds on the Orkney Islands, and even more when you count the occasional visitors?"

"You have mentioned it," she said dryly.

"It's an ornithologist's paradise, all right," her mother said enthusiastically. "The flat limestone beds weather into ideal ledges for nest building, and the moorlands support an amazing variety of raptors."

Jamie wasn't even interested enough to say something sarcastic.

Her room was bitterly cold when she went upstairs. She rummaged in her bag for a nightgown, but the one she found clearly wasn't warm enough. Her parents had warned her to pack warm things, but that had been hard to do when it was already getting hot and humid back home. After a quick dash to the bathroom and a battle with the uncooperative plumbing, she leaped into bed wearing both nightgown and bathrobe and pulled the down-filled comforter up to her chin. Too cold to even think of sleeping, she watched a patch of moonlight slide slowly over the flowered wallpaper.

Cold moonlight shining on a barren island in the middle of a dark icy sea. Her brother was probably seeing the same moonlight pouring over a warm tropical sea as he walked with friends in soft sands and breathed

perfumes from exotic flowers. How could he have everything—all the talent, all the prospects, all the luck?
Her "spring break" promised to be an ordeal, and the
chances of using it to prove her one natural talent were
looking grim.

She woke up in the dead of night. Her body still
seemed to be on U.S. time and was giving her all the
wrong signals. The moon patch had moved from wall to
ceiling, but there was no change in the ceaseless blowing of the wind. She felt fully awake. Should she read
one of the stack of ghost stories she'd brought along?

No, that'd be admitting defeat. Here she was in the
middle of the night in a 300-year-old Scottish house. No
matter what the rental agent said, this place must have
a filmy lady in white or some gaunt tormented specter
floating about. Not everyone was as sensitive as she
was. They couldn't see those things, that was all.

If she was going to ghost-hunt, though, Jamie decided, she'd better take along a camera as backup. She'd
read that sometimes ghosts invisible to the human eye
could be captured on film.

Climbing from her now warm cocoon of a bed, she
quickly pulled on jeans, sweater, jacket, and sneakers.
Then, grabbing up camera and flashlight, she tiptoed
out onto the landing.

Her father's steady snoring rumbled from the other
front bedroom, but otherwise the only sound was the
wind playing roughly with the roof slates. The landing
did not look promisingly ghostly.

Putting her hand to the knob of the unoccupied bedroom, Jamie dramatically flung open the door. The
window was a pale smudge of light in the far wall, but

even in the misty moonlight there were no filmy shapes,
no mysterious lights. It didn't feel even vaguely eerie. It
was just an unused, cold, and slightly damp bedroom.
Without much hope, she took a couple of flash pictures
and returned to the landing.

Well, that was just one room.

Slowly Jamie crept downstairs. What with the noise
of the wind and her father's snoring, she could have
charged down, but tiptoeing was what one did in a
haunted house.

She slipped into each room, stood silently, and tried
to sense supernatural vibrations. Nothing. All Jamie
felt was cold: not the soul-chilling cold of the grave, but
just plain cold. She'd flick on her flashlight and check
the walls hoping to spot secret passages that had been
walled over, tormented skeletons trapped behind. Nothing but smooth cheery wallpaper. Methodically she
took pictures, convinced that she was wasting film.

People didn't call her stubborn for nothing, she told
herself. There was still the outside.

Easing open the back door, Jamie slipped out. The
wind battered her with cold, but with no particular
sense of evil. In the low moonlight, the house cast an
inky shadow over the backyard. Promising. But
through it, there wafted no pale woman in white. Big
surprise, Jamie thought disgustedly. In this climate, nobody, alive *or* dead, would waft around in filmy white
draperies.

Taking pictures, she walked to the dilapidated stone
outbuildings and shone her light inside. An old carriage
house, without the faintest outline of ghostly carriages
or misty white mares. Just a sawhorse, some lumber,

and a jumble of old tools. Thoroughly annoyed, she tromped around the house to the front yard.

Pale, shivering shapes were moonlit daffodils twisting in the wind. Jamie glared up at the old house. Its bland stone face slept contentedly. The dark windows opened onto no terrible secrets. The splotches on wall and roof were lichen, not blood. The —

Something white wavered on the peak of the roof, glimmering in the moonlight. It shifted, changed shape, and floated through the air toward her. In sudden terror, Jamie crouched on the grass. With a mournful cry, the thing sailed over her head, glaring at her with ice-blue eyes. Then it swooped over the wall and landed on the tall stone in the pasture across the road. Trembling, Jamie stood as the thing settled its silvered shape onto the stone. Again, it cried into the night.

An owl.

Her parents could probably tell her what kind of owl. Big and white, with blue eyes and a cry like a soul in torment. But just a dumb bird! With a final cry, it flew off westward over the fields.

Angrily, Jamie snapped a few pictures in the yard and stomped back toward the house. All this spooky atmosphere, and the only thing that frightened her was a stupid owl!

No, that wasn't true, she admitted when she stepped inside, out of the wind. There was another tiny fear growing in her. A fear that even if this place was filled with things supernatural, she would not know it. A fear that maybe she was no good at this either.

No, no, no! she felt like screaming to the dark,

placid house. This *was* her talent. She just had to find the right place to practice it. And Jamie Halcro was never one to give up. She had two weeks on this wretched island, and if it held one shred of a ghost, she would find it!

Chapter Three

At least the cupboard's stocked with marmalade," Mr. Halcro said, plunking a jar onto the table. "The staple of the English breakfast."

"That, and frying everything in a lake of grease," his wife added.

Bundled up in the chilly dining room, Jamie was not interested in the breakfast habits of the British, only in their haunting habits—or lack thereof.

She had roughly shoved away last night's doubts and was now forming a battle plan. But the failure of her first effort still annoyed her, as did the fact that the only thing that had sent shivers up her spine was a stupid blue-eyed bird landing on a tall rock.

She glanced out the window at the gray wind-churned morning. The top of that tall stone was just visible beyond their wall, taunting her. "Why did they bother to set up that big rock in the pasture over there?" she asked sharply as she spread marmalade on toast. "Just as a sheep back-scratcher?"

Her father followed her gaze out the window. "The standing stone there? No, that's really ancient. That's one of the things these islands are noted for: their Neolithic monuments. Our guidebooks say that this stone is part of a whole chain of standing stones and stone circles leading across the middle part of the island. They're supposed to be about five thousand years old."

"What did they set them up for?"

"No one knows for sure, except that it was probably something astronomical, lining up with sunrises and eclipses and such—like Stonehenge in England."

"Oh. So they're not gravestones or anything?"

"No; more like temples, I guess."

With a discouraged shrug, Jamie turned to her canned peaches. For a moment, she'd thought that the reason the owl and stone had seemed so creepy was that there was really some sort of ancient cemetery out there and that she'd been picking up ghostly vibrations. So much for that theory.

Sitting across from her, Jamie's mother was jotting down a list on the back of an old envelope. "Sorry, no birding excursions, Doug, until we go into town and stock up on groceries. You'll want to come too, Jamie. Kirkwall's supposed to be an interesting town, and the bus line stops right by this house, so you can go in on your own later if you don't want to go birding with us."

"Got that right," Jamie muttered. How, she wondered for the thousandth time, could two grown people get such a kick out of sitting still for hours watching birds? She considered asking them what sort of local white owl had blue eyes, but thought better of it. They'd probably tell her at great length.

In the car on the way to town, Jamie's father lectured on the variety of seagulls that could be found in the Orkneys, and then slid into a discussion of the local economy. "Beats me how folks ever made much of a living here. Sheep and fish mostly. One of the big exports seems to have been dried seaweed. It's no wonder my ancestors cleared out."

His wife laughed. "The way you used to go on about it made it sound as if your ancestors held grand estates in the Scottish isles."

"Nothing of the sort," he said indignantly. "All I knew was that my ancestors emigrated from the Orkney Islands a couple of hundred years ago. Of course, I may have embroidered the details just a little."

Jamie had been half listening, half watching the landscape. They came to a small town, just a cluster of houses really, with a church and cemetery. For a moment she was afraid that this was the big town of Kirkwall. But they drove on through.

When they did get to the capital of the Orkney Islands, it didn't seem much bigger. There was a little harbor smelling of sea, oil, and coal smoke, and back from the water were several shopping streets. In addition to the few grocery stores and bakeries, there were numerous shops apparently dedicated to selling toy puffins, jewelry, and wool sweaters to tourists.

These streets also seemed the place for the local teenagers to hang out, flaunting their toughness in the cold by wearing jeans and tank tops. Jamie could feel them looking her over and pegging her by her stylish warm clothes as a clueless tourist. She blushed with resentment until she thought about how awful it would be to be stuck here year round. What was there to do besides watch puffins and bother tourists? Good thing her father's family had got up and gone.

In the center of the town stood a red stone cathedral surrounded by an old-looking cemetery. This might be a place to try and scare up some ghosts, but would any hang around a busy town square with cars and trucks rumbling by? Maybe the little cemetery they'd passed on the way would do better.

When they had finally finished shopping and were heading back, Jamie suggested they drop her off at the village so she could do some walking and exploring.

"You don't want to go to Deerness and look for guillemots?" her mother chuckled. "Well, I suppose there are worse forms of teenage rebellion than rejecting birds."

"Mother!" Jamie objected. "It's not the birds I mind, it's the hours spent watching them. They've got enough sense not to sit around and watch us, after all."

Her father sighed theatrically. "Well, at least take this guidebook and map so you can figure out what you're seeing and how to get back."

Once they'd let her off, Jamie stuffed the guidebook and map into one of her pockets and walked toward the church and its little walled cemetery.

Opening the creaking iron gate, she slipped in. It was a lot quieter here than in town. Other than the wind, she heard only a few droning cars and an occasional distant voice or barking dog. Much better for ghosts.

Systematically she walked up and down the ragged rows of tombstones, taking pictures but feeling nothing—not the faintest twinge of the supernatural. The only thing that startled her was suddenly seeing her own last name on a tombstone. Halcro. Then she found several other Halcros scattered about. So her father's family had come from around here. Good. Maybe if she had some kind of link, the ghosts would be more cooperative.

She sat on the grass beside the lichen-splotched stone of Duncan Halcro. The writing was worn, but the dates looked like "1706–1753." She closed her eyes, spread her hands over the grass, and felt—nothing. Minutes passed. Still nothing. Whatever had happened to Duncan Halcro in 1753, it hadn't left him an unquiet spirit waiting to be summoned by some distant descendant.

Discouraged, Jamie got up and walked away from the headstones to sit on the cold stone steps of the little church. Searching her pockets for a candy bar, she found the map and guidebook and pulled them out.

Halfheartedly she flipped open the guidebook. Now, where else might she find ghosts? This whole island seemed to be dotted with "megalithic chambered cairns": earth-covered stone tombs where the people of 5,000 years ago buried their dead. One of the cairns, Maes Howe, was considered the best example of this sort of thing in all of Europe. There was also an admission price and a guide to take you through it.

Forget that. Jamie doubted any 5,000-year-old

ghost would hang out in a tourist trap. But according to the guidebook, there were also smaller cairns around the countryside that people could just walk into if they wanted. Maybe she'd have better luck there.

Unfolding the map, she studied it for a while and finally found where she was, a village with a "cemy" marked beside it. Kind of a cheery abbreviation for a usually gloomy sort of place. She also found several cairns marked on the nearby hills. Jamie looked up from the map. Gray and windy, not exactly a great day for a walk, but so far that seemed the only kind of weather they had here. A walk sounded better than hanging around a totally unhaunted house all afternoon.

At a small corner store Jamie bought a meat pie and a soda for lunch; then she set off along the road shown on the map. She passed a few modern houses, but the rest were old ones built of gray stone. The only color in the landscape came from nodding daffodils and laundry on clotheslines flapping in the constant wind. The hills were all gray-green or purple-brown heather. Her dad said that heather in bloom was a beautiful bright purple. April was obviously not the month it bloomed.

The higher she climbed, the fewer the houses. Sheep grazed behind stone walls, and the wind filled the air with a steady dry roar. The tops of the hills had disappeared in cloud, not fluffy white but a frayed blanket of gray.

She stopped and struggled with the wind to unfold the map. Already she seemed to have missed the turnoff to one cairn, but there should be another one ahead. On the ground, these roads certainly didn't look the way they did on the map. Jamie trudged on, getting hungry but refusing to stop and eat until she had reached her goal.

At last she came to a parking lot where a small sign marked "Chambered Cairn" pointed to a path. It was narrow, little more than a sheep track worn in the springy ground. Peat, Jamie guessed. Weren't peat bogs like quicksand, the kind of place people sank into and were never heard of again? She kept carefully to the path and watched for the white wooden arrows marking the way.

The path slanted down the hillside. Above, the clouds were creeping lower, but below she could see headlands, bays, and the silver sweep of ocean. The only sounds were the wind and the cry of birds riding upon it.

Where was this wretched cairn? If she wanted an out-of-the-way grave site, this certainly was it. The little arrows kept urging her on. Then the path split. One fork angled up, disappearing into cloud, but the lower one led to a distant rectangle of fence surrounding a hump of earth. She grunted. This had better be good.

When she finally reached the entrance to the tomb, Jamie realized that the guidebook's phrase "walk in and visit on your own" hadn't been quite right. "Walk in" if you were a foot high, maybe.

A little grilled gate closed off the entrance. She tugged on it and it creaked open. Good sound effects.

The low passage was made of large stone slabs forming the walls, floor, and ceiling. At the entrance, a few black slugs slithered slowly across the stone. Trying not to squash them, Jamie got on her hands and knees and started crawling. Her body blocked out most of the light. Suppose the passage ahead dropped into a pit, she thought suddenly with a jolt of fear that had nothing to do with ghosts. She didn't mind tight places, but she really hated heights and even the thought of falling. Still, she wouldn't give up now.

Carefully she inched forward. The stones were cold and slick with dampness. After maybe eight feet, she could feel the space open out around her. Cautiously she lifted her head. Weak gray light filtered through a hole in the ceiling, now ten feet above. Slowly her eyes made out a stone-paved floor and walls of stacked stone that gradually slanted inward until they formed the roof. She also saw, resting on the floor, a yellow flashlight with some government logo stamped on it.

Gratefully Jamie grabbed it up and by its weak beam made out patches of deeper darkness in the walls, entrances to low side chambers. No way she'd crawl into those and maybe get stuck. She switched off the light, leaned against the cold walls, and tried to pick up ghostly vibrations.

After ten minutes, all she felt was cold and hunger. From her jacket pocket, she pulled the soda and slightly squashed pie. Luncheon in a 5,000-year-old tomb. Weird. She frowned. "Weird" as in "offbeat," not as in "creepy." She felt cold, cramped, and kind of closed in, yes, but she didn't feel a whiff of fear. This was just the sort of place fantasy writers described. But where were the wispy wraiths, the grasping skeletal hands? The only ghostly things she'd seen were little black slugs.

Wadding up the pie wrappers, she jammed them into a pocket and pulled out her camera. In the sharp sudden light of the flash, the dark recesses and shadowy stone walls became clear, close, and even more un-spooky.

Closing her eyes, Jamie tried again to sense that she was surrounded by something other than cold, lifeless air and piled-up stone. With her feelings, she reached and reached until she touched a chill, spreading fear. The same fear she'd felt before, but it had grown. The fear that her one talent was just an empty hope, a grasping for worth where there was none. Heavy and cold, the fear spread through her.

No! She knew she was right. It was the place that was wrong. It was *too* old. Wind and rain had scoured away the ancient spirits centuries ago. But surely somewhere on this island conditions were right for ghosts. There must be something, other than a stupid nagging doubt, to be frightened of.

Angrily Jamie crouched down and began crawling back out the low, dank passage. She moved too fast, but ignored the scrapes and bruises. At last she edged past the rusty gate and stood up.

Suddenly she was very frightened indeed.

Chapter Four

The world was gone. A few feet in front of her there was nothing but gray. Grayness in all directions. It was like in one of those books. She'd gone through a door in her world and come out in another. In a world of gray nothing.

It was gray and wet, like mist. Like a *cloud*, that was all! The cloud had crept farther down the hill while she'd been inside the cairn. Around her, the usual raging wind was muffled into a ghostly sigh.

Jamie felt a quick surge of relief, but it just as quickly faded. In this mist, she'd have a hard time finding the path back. She thought of that Sherlock Holmes story about a ghostly hound in which someone strays off a misty path and gets sucked into the mire.

She'd left the government flashlight back in the tomb, but it was too weak to do much good here. With her eyes on the ground a few feet ahead, she slowly set

out, trying to remember her route. Past the gate, turn
right. Go uphill.

For a while the path was clear enough, cutting
through peat, heather, and coarse curly grass. Sometimes where the ground was boggy, the path braided,
but the strands always came back together. Once, taking a branch that petered out, she had to backtrack to
the other. A white wooden arrow solidifying out of the
mist showed she was right.

Instead of thinning, the mist seemed to be getting
denser. A white wall of silence bounded her world,
shrinking it to a few feet of boggy hillside. Then Jamie
realized she had lost the path altogether. She'd side-
stepped around a particularly muddy patch, and now
there was nothing in sight but untrampled heather.

Panic seeped like cold from the ground. This wasn't
some half-remembered story read in the warmth of her
room. It was real, it was now, and *she* was the person
wandering lost. Frantically Jamie stumbled about,
looking for the trail.

There it was, a little trench of hard earth cut through
the heather. Swiftly and gratefully she followed it, eager
to be free of this nightmare. But the trail led on and on
and didn't rise when she thought it should. And there
were no helpful white arrows along the way. At last
Jamie admitted this was just a sheep trail.

But surely she couldn't be too far from some road or
farm by now. She called out a hello. The sound fell to
the ground, heavy and muffled. She tried again, but the
blanketing mist soaked up the words almost as soon as
they left her mouth.

Jamie strained her ears. Had that been an answer?

She called out again, and again came an answering call. She looked around, straining to see through the mist.

"Where are you?" No answer, but she saw a smudge of darkness in the mist ahead. With a sigh of relief, Jamie stumbled forward.

Again she called. Still no answer, but the shape seemed clearer. It was moving along the same path as she. Another hiker? Putting on speed, she tried to catch up. She could see more clearly now. He or she was short. A child? Closer, and the moving object was taking shape. A wide, four-legged shape. It was a sheep.

In shock, Jamie stopped and stared. The sheep stopped too, gazing back at her with calm blue eyes. Then it turned and trotted on ahead.

What choice had she now? Shrugging, she followed. Even sheep go somewhere.

Her woolly guide faded in and out of the mist but always stayed enough in sight to keep Jamie on the trail. Slowly other vague shapes began to form through the mist — a fence post, a stunted hedge.

Then suddenly she had stepped below the cloud. The island, sea, and inland loch spread out before her. In the west, other clouds had folded themselves along the horizon. At that moment, two slid apart, loosing a shaft of sunlight onto the landscape below. In a golden river, it slid across the fields. That house on the edge of the light, surely that was hers. Yes, across from it was the lone standing stone. And from here, Jamie could see the chain of stones and stone circles that were clearly linked to it. Together they glowed in that path of light.

She laughed with relief, and in front of her the sheep bleated. It gave her another blue-eyed stare, then trotted quickly down the hillside. Happily Jamie ran after it, but she didn't need a four-footed guide anymore. The ground was firm, and she could see her goal. She stopped once, exuberantly taking a picture, then hurried on. When she turned to wave to her guide, it was gone, probably settled into the grass somewhere.

By the time Jamie got home it was early evening, but her parents weren't back yet. They'd stay out watching birds until last light, she knew. Exhausted, she went upstairs and changed out of her dank, stained clothes.

Looking out her window, she saw that the clouds had closed in on the sun again, but she could clearly see the tall dark stone standing alone in the field. In her mind, Jamie again saw the pattern which it and the other stones had made, linked together in that golden path of light.

The picture brought an odd tugging into her mind. Uneasily she tried to shake it away. It seemed to be tugging toward something dark and dangerous — something that reminded her of how, as a little kid, she'd played she had supernatural powers, until that horrible time when one of them seemed to work. She'd been wrong, of course. Surely she hadn't been able to move that glass with her mind, but the chasm that the moment had shown her had been deep and frightening.

Jamie shook her head firmly. No, it definitely wasn't make-believe powers or mysterious ancient stones that interested her. It was ghosts. The ghost of some fallen soldier or murdered heiress — a spirit she had a special talent to see, a spirit she could link to some real, under-standable past. If she could just crank out a little more patience, she knew she'd find it.

The next morning it was raining. Not a gentle rain, but rain that the wind snatched up and hurled like BBs against the windowpanes. Her parents postponed their birding plans for the day and decided to go into town to look at the museum. Jamie chose to stay behind and delve into the suitcaseful of ghost sto-ries she'd brought along. To use up her film, she took one last picture out her window into the rain, then sent the roll with her parents, hoping they'd find a quick developer. Kirkwall was a tourist town, after all.

The book she started was pretty good, but Jamie had trouble getting into it. A couple of kids whose teacher's house was haunted were trying to help him find where the ghost's unburied bones were. What an-noyed her was reading about this sort of thing when she should be living it. When her parents returned, she was in a thoroughly rotten mood, but hope soared again when they handed her a packet of developed photos.

Charging up the stairs, Jamie plunked onto her squeaky bed and tore open the packet. She flipped through the photos, each one driving her a little further into gloom. The spare room, the kitchen, the parlor: all perfectly ordinary rooms. Not one misty shape where nothing should have been, not one unexplained shadow. The outside pictures hadn't even captured the windy wild-ness of the night. The only touch of quirkiness was where the flash had reflected in blue glints from the eyes of the owl perched on the standing stone. It gave her a moment's shiver, but it was nothing. She got a similar effect when she took a picture of her cat at home.

The cemetery pictures were just as useless: no glowing inscriptions on the stones, no pale auras lingering over the grass. The shots on the foggy hillside were a total washout, and the inside of the burial cairn looked like a cozy stone house.

At the next picture, she gasped. Nothing supernatural, but a good picture. No, a great one—like a professional postcard shot. It was taken from the hillside, looking over shadowed fields to a slate-gray sea. Mountainous clouds were slashed by a chasm of light, and through it a stream of sunlight poured across the island, highlighting the chain of ancient stones. The one flaw was that the sheep in the foreground had caught the light so that its eyes looked like two glowing blue marbles. Weird, but just another trick of the light.

She sighed, tossing the snapshot onto her bed. The only good picture, and it *would* be of those wretched stones. The glowing blue aura in the last photo gave her a brief surge of hope, but it was just the reflection of the flash in her window. Fuzzily, through it and the rain, she could make out the standing stone with another stupid bird on top. Great, a clean sweep. A hundred-percent waste of film!

Smoldering, she stomped downstairs.

Two days later Jamie had read most of the books she'd brought and, out of intense boredom, had agreed to go birding with her parents. On the drive to the island's west coast, she paid little attention to their bird chatter. When they finally parked the car and all started crossing a field, she fell behind, stopping to watch some cows grazing. She found them impressively big.

Looking up, Jamie realized that her parents had disappeared over the top of a hill. She plodded after them. The hill sloped up steeply, giving the feeling of climbing right into the cloud-racked sky. She reached the top and gasped. There was nothing below.

Ten feet in front of her, the land dropped abruptly away. In the distance beyond, gray sky and sea almost blended together. At the base of the cliff, she could hear surf pounding onto rocks.

Her fear of heights hit with the same force as the wind, and she staggered back. Crouching down against both, she clutched the grass and dizzily scanned the clifftop for her parents. She spotted them, in their turquoise jackets, some thirty feet away. They were lying on their stomachs above a narrow cove, studying the opposite cliff with binoculars. Fighting back queasiness, she crawled along the ridge to join them.

"Careful of those burrows," her mother yelled over the wind, pointing to small dark holes slanting into the sandy earth. "They're mostly old rabbit burrows—the puffins use them as nests during the summer. It's still early for puffins, but there are some great gannets over there."

Jamie was handed the binoculars and dutifully looked through them at some long-necked white birds with dirty-yellow heads. Big deal. Actually she wouldn't half mind seeing some puffins—funny fat bouncy birds with huge, colorful beaks. She sighed. It was too much to ask to have any birds about worth looking at.

She handed the glasses back to her mother and, using her parents as windbreaks, snuggled into the sand and grass. Maybe she could imagine being a puffin tucked into its burrow. No, she wouldn't even *imagine* being that close to a cliff edge. How about flat beaches instead? Flat, warm, sunny beaches. Flamingos flying over. Palm trees swaying in a soft quiet breeze.

She managed to drift into sleep, but the rain awakened her. It started as big heavy drops, splashing little craters in the sandy soil. Then the drops became smaller and harder. They bounced off the ground like tiny marbles. Hail.

"Back to the car," her father said. Jamie couldn't believe the reluctance in his voice, but she jumped up and tore down the slope, past the grazing cows, and into the car. When her parents joined her, she found their conversation equally hard to believe.

"It'll pass over soon," her mother assured them. "There's a major seabird sanctuary marked farther down the coast. Let's head there."

Stifling a groan, Jamie said, "Sounds delightful, but could you drop me off at the house first?"

"That's a bit out of our way," her mother commented.

Her father was studying the map. "How about a compromise? It looks as if we can take this road and let you off where it crosses this other one. Then it's a straight walk back to the house. Kind of a long one, but the hail's stopped and the day's still young."

"Yeah, fine," Jamie agreed. Anything but more birds.

When she stepped from the car at the crossroads the wind hit again, but already the sky's gray cloak was tearing and blue was showing through. Recalling the map, she turned east and headed down the road, stepping to the grassy verge whenever a car passed.

The way ahead was obvious even without a map. A single road dipped to where two lochs pinched closer and closer until the land was only a narrow strip. When the land broadened out again, the road would lead almost directly to their house.

Abruptly Jamie stopped. She remembered something else, not from the map but from the view two nights earlier from the other side of this valley. This route also followed the chain of ancient standing stones and circles she had seen spotlighted after the sheep led her from the mist.

She suddenly felt angry and oddly afraid. Every time she turned around, there were those stones again—birds perching on them, sheep pointing them out—and now her only route home passed by them. It was almost as if she was supposed to go there. She turned a shiver into an angry shrug. Jamie Halcro was not the sort of person who liked to be told where to go!

With an annoyed laugh, she started walking again. The stones kept showing up because there happened to be a lot of them around here. A lot more stones than ghosts, that was for sure. But if a search for ghosts didn't scare her, why should a few old stones?

The sun was making her feel better. On both sides of the road, the lochs were a sparkling blue, and the wind had dropped from a gale to a strong breeze. Overhead, it rolled billowy white clouds across a blue sky, casting a moving pattern of cloud shadows over the fields and the sweep of darker hills. What Jamie at first thought were whitecaps on the water turned out to be swans—wild swans, not the tame type people threw breadcrumbs to in parks.

Ahead and to the right, she could see what must be a stone circle. Again a twinge of fear jabbed her, but she pushed it down. This was one of the things people came here to see. What could be the harm in walking past it?

The closer she got, the more impressive the circle seemed. It was larger than she'd imagined, maybe 300 feet across, and the stones—big irregular slabs—were taller. Some were missing, but it was easy to tell where they had stood to complete the circle.

Now she was passing the gate of the fenced-off enclosure. Across the road was a small parking lot with a few cars, but there were no guides or admission takers at the gate. She really ought to go in, she told herself. It was supposed to be a big local deal, and she was right here. At the same time, a nagging fear whispered that she shouldn't do what everything had been pushing her to do.

Well, I won't be pushed around by stupid nameless fears either, she said to herself, and walked through the gate.

Briefly she joined a pair of Asian tourists at several information plaques. This circle, a little younger than one farther up the road, dated from the third millennium B.C. That was old. And like her dad said, no one was quite sure why such circles were built, except that the purpose was probably religious or astronomical. A second plaque went on at length about keeping to the paths so the "natural heather mat" could be reestablished. Jamie followed the path across a deep ditch to the circle itself.

The stones almost all towered over her. Wide and flat, they were broken at the top into sharp angles, looking like large, rotting teeth. The thought made her shiver again. Deliberately she walked up to a stone twice her height and gingerly touched it. Its surface was smoother than she'd expected, like fine sandpaper, and the reddish gray was flecked with specks of glitter and splotched with lichen—irregular patches of white, orange, yellow, and even pale blue. It was also warm, as though greedily soaking up the rare sunshine. For a while she stood on the stone's sunny side, letting its broad shape shield her from the wind.

Then, slowly, Jamie began walking around the circle, following the path of mown grass just inside the stones. The inner part of the circle was covered with low purplish heather. She wondered what the circle looked like from the center.

She veered from the path only to find a small insistent white sign at her feet—Keep to the Perimeter Path—fussily protecting the precious heather mat.

No one was going to tell her where to walk! For crying out loud, half the island was covered with heather. Jamie teetered forward, wanting desperately to walk to the center of the circle. Another force just as desperately wanted her to pull back, to leave the center to its heather—to leave the whole circle alone. It urged her to run out the gate and down the road, not stopping until she had closed herself behind walls and doors.

In the back of her mind, Jamie knew that what scared her most was that she should care so violently either way. The Orkney police wouldn't arrest her if she stepped on the stupid heather. On the other hand, she could just as easily be like other tourists and see the circle from the "perimeter path." What was the big deal?

She didn't know. But suddenly she knew it *was* big, and she didn't want any part of it.

But it wanted her. She felt as if dry invisible hands were clutching her, dragging her into the center of the circled stones.

Chapter Five

S tubbornly, violently Jamie jerked back. She staggered and almost lost her footing. A couple of
tourists stared at her oddly and walked on. She
couldn't even flash them a sheepish grin. All she could
do was turn and run.

She ran out to the road and jogged eastward along
its verge. The land narrowed to a slim causeway between the lochs, then spread out again. Averting her
eyes, she jogged past the remains of a smaller stone circle on her left. Finally she slowed to a walk, but
pointedly ignored the standing stone across from their
house. Going directly to her room, she closed the curtain, threw herself on the bed, and started reading a
book she'd read four times before.

As the afternoon passed and her mind thawed out,
Jamie began to feel really foolish. How could she have
been so silly? Why had she felt so strongly about a

really unimportant thing? What difference did it make if she walked on the stupid heather or not?

Anyway, it was a dumb rule and a dumb sign, and the rule makers and sign posters ought to have people walking on their heather all the time just to tell them so.

When her parents came home, they were full of talk about the afternoon's birds, so Jamie didn't have to mention the stone circle. It wasn't really important anyway. In fact, now she could hardly remember what her problem had been with it. Just anger, she guessed, anger at those fussy Orkney tourist people and their stupid prissy rules. Rules like that were meant to be broken. Like Wet Cement and Keep Off the Grass signs, they were outright invitations.

She played with that thought all the way through dinner, and it cheered her up a lot. By bedtime, it was a warm bubbly idea, and she didn't have to wait long to put it into practice.

She opened her curtain. The moon was fuller than before, and the sky was free of even the faintest cloud. The standing stone across the road stretched its long shadow toward her. But stones were nothing. What she was after was heather.

Once again, Jamie waited until her parents were asleep. Lying on her bed fully clothed, she refused to listen to any conflicting mental voices. This was *her* idea, a good one, and she would carry it out. When snores began to fill the house, she crept down the stairs and out the front door.

No sooner was she outside than a great white owl

called from its perch on the standing stone. Jamie tried to calm her jolting heart. So the big, blue-eyed owl was on the stone again. All that meant was that lots of mice ran around this field at night. Resolutely, Jamie marched along the road, keeping her mind focused on the heather and the pleasure of defying that petty busybody rule.

And anyway, it was a beautiful night for a walk. Windy, of course, but she was warmly dressed, and this far from city lights the stars were wonderfully bright. A half moon silvered the waves, spread a sheen over the grass, and cast sharp-edged shadows from fence posts and the first circle of standing stones. She strode by it and the next single standing stone.

Where the road narrowed, she looked down at both shores and saw the white forms of sleeping swans. One swan raised its head and watched her pass, but sounded no alarm.

Jamie neared the big stone circle and slowed. Her conviction that this was a great idea was beginning to fade. Maybe it was kind of silly. But, hey, here she was, and she might as well go through with it. If there was one thing she hated more than looking silly, it was starting something and then giving up. She turned off the road, passed the information placards, and crossed the ditch by the earth causeway.

Again, she slowed. There was the heather before her, a pure untrampled field of it. On both sides curved the stones, towering over her like dark misshapen guards. And again came the odd, cold conviction that the center of the circle was exactly where something wanted her to be.

Nonsense! Nobody cared about the center of this circle except the people who put up those prissy Keep to the Perimeter Path signs. No way would they cow her! The only place to see a circle was from the center. With a defiant yell, Jamie stepped off the path and onto the heather.

Another step and another. She walked, then ran forward. Underfoot, the heather was dry and springy, a crunchy pleasure. Jamie reached the center, threw wide her arms, and slowly spun around.

This really did seem the center of things. Beyond the circling stones, water and land stretched out in all directions until they met sky. Throwing back her head, Jamie gazed upward. As she turned, the stars seemed to turn around her. Arms outstretched, eyes on the stars, she turned faster and faster. The stars spun in a dizzying swirl. Faster, and faster yet, until they blended into a blinding curtain of light.

Then an explosion of blackness.

Time, Jamie knew, had passed. Time spent in silence and utter darkness. Slowly she pushed herself up from the ground, from the crackly, springy heather. Fighting dizziness, she looked up and had to jam her eyes shut. The stars burned like ice, far harder and brighter than before. It was as if the atmosphere had burned off, leaving nothing but the cold infinite universe.

Keeping her eyes low, she opened them again. The stones still stood around her, but they were different, too. There were more of them, forming an unbroken

circle. And for the first time since coming to these islands, she could not hear the wind. There was utter silence.

In rising terror, Jamie scrambled to her feet, then
immediately crouched again. A dark shape loomed
above her. It seemed to have arms, a head, a voice.

"Taken your time, haven't you?" the man said impatiently. "And taken mine as well. That first boy knew
the power and wanted it, and the second didn't even
know what it was. But you knew just enough to be
afraid and fight it every step of the way. What a
bother!"

Then came a dry cold laugh. "But no matter, you're
all here now. So come, you three, stop cowering in the
heather. I'll light a fire and we can talk."

Surprised, Jamie noticed two other figures huddled
on the ground nearby. Slowly both stood up, and the
taller one spoke.

"Sir, I have no intention of sitting and talking with
an obviously hostile native. I demand that you shut off
this effect and let me return to my ship and complete
my Nri Irll."

The man only grunted. He walked to a bare spot
in the heather and clapped his hands; a lively campfire
suddenly appeared on the ground. For a moment, its
crackling was the only sound in the total stillness.

"Fire!" the smaller figure said, running toward it.
"You can make fire by magic?"

"Of course. It's one of the basics."

In the firelight, Jamie could now see those two
clearly. The man was short and dark, his curly black
hair and beard shot with gray. He was wearing leather

trousers and a long cloak of slick dark fur. The boy was young. The hood of his woven yellow cape had fallen back to show a mop of red hair.

The other figure strode toward them, and Jamie stared. His skin was dark, but not in the way she was used to. It was more the color of old avocados, a greenish brown. His hair was not just black. It was a glossy *blue*-black, and it bristled in a crest over his head to trail down his back like a mane. He was wearing boots and a coppery-colored jumpsuit.

"You have no right to hold me here," he said angrily, "and I am not interested in your petty holographic illusions. I demand that you let down the force field you have around this place and let me go."

"No time for argument, boy. Sit down, we need to talk."

"You can not order me around. I am Kreeth. I have permission to be on this island and—"

"No," the man interrupted, "you are not Kreeth. You are part Human—*my* part. And here, Tyaak, all the rights are on my side." Abruptly he turned and addressed the other boy. "And you—your name is Arni."

"Arni Arnorson," the younger boy said eagerly. "My father is Arnor, skald to Earl Thorfinn."

The man nodded, then looked up. "And you, Jamie, come join us. I've had enough trouble with you already."

Confused, angry, and terribly afraid, Jamie walked toward the fire. She decided to hide everything but the anger. "Mister, I have no idea who you are, how you know my name, or what is going on here, but—"

"Then sit down, and I'll tell you."

"But—"

"Sit!"

Jamie found herself sitting on the heather. The two called Tyaak and Arni were sitting as well, with surprised looks on their faces. The man stared down at them with cold blue eyes; then he, too, sat.

"My name is Urkar. I am your great-great-great-whatever—your ancestor, anyway. And that is why you are here. Ours is a family of power. It is strong in me, and it is strong in each one of you."

Arni's face lit up. "You mean I *do* have the power, like Great-grandmother Eithne? I always knew it! I always knew I could work magic!"

"Magic?" Tyaak objected. "What sort of superstitious babble is this? Backwater planet that it may be, I thought Earth was at least advanced enough to forget that foolishness."

"In your time, unfortunately, it *has* forgotten magic," Urkar growled. "But forgetting something doesn't make it not exist. Now, stop interrupting me.

"Where was I? Yes, descendants. For millennia, every member of our line has inherited some degree of power. Many never used or even recognized it. Others channeled it into certain trades or skills. But all three of you are especially strong carriers of the power, and you also live in especially critical times—times when you are called upon to use it."

"I am sorry," Tyaak said, standing up. "Not only are you ridiculous, you are wrong. I have no 'magic powers.' The only thing I am called upon to do is complete my Nri Irll and—"

"Do shut up!" Urkar snapped, and abruptly Tyaak

was sitting again. Strange-looking as the boy was, Jamie could recognize the anger and confusion in his face. His expression, she was sure, mirrored her own.

She cleared her throat uncertainly. "I don't know about these two, but I *certainly* don't have any magic powers. I always thought I could sense the supernatural, but it turns out I can't. I've been trying hard, and I haven't seen one ghost yet."

"Ghosts!" Urkar sputtered. "Just what do you think the 'supernatural' is? It's simply power that goes beyond the common laws of nature. Making use of this power is what you call magic. And seeing ghosts is only a tiny passive sideline of that."

Jamie sat silent for a moment, letting this settle through her mind, rearranging things.

Arni spoke up again. "These two must come from some pretty strange places not to know about magic. But what do you mean, Urkar, about being called upon to use it?"

The man combed a hand through his gray-streaked hair. "I'd better explain about power first. I imagine that even Tyaak understands about there being two kinds of it in the universe."

"Two kinds?" the boy said. "You mean like matter and antimatter?"

"Something like I suppose. In the universe there are two forces, one that creates and one that destroys. Usually they are in balance, but occasionally one force grows and breaks over the other like a storm. If it is the creative force, then a rash of new mountains or worlds or galaxies can be created. If the storm is one of destruction, then mountains, planets, and galaxies can be destroyed."

Tyaak sneered. "Sounds like superstitious clothing over basic cosmic dynamics—energy rift theory gone wild. But what does this have to—"

"Stop interrupting, and I'll tell you. Throughout the universe, there are beings who can sense these forces and use them, gravitating either to the destructive or the creative. When a force storm looms up, those of the threatened side use their powers to resist."

Arni was frowning. "What sort of power does our family have?"

"Creative."

"Good. I don't think I'd much like doing evil magic."

"Evil magic!" Tyaak exploded. "I have had quite enough!"

"No you haven't!" Urkar stabbed him with his icy blue gaze. " 'Evil' is one term for it. So is 'destruction,' or 'chaos,' or 'death,' or—what did you call it?— antimatter.

"Now, I *will* continue. One of those storms of destruction was growing when I was a young man. On these islands, we had always tried to channel and strengthen our forces through constructs of power, the way pillars and roof posts are repaired or added when a great storm is brewing out at sea. But this storm was greater than any ever faced before. Those of us who wielded power determined that a new central pillar of creative force was needed to, so to speak, keep the roof on this part of the universe from collapsing."

Urkar stood, sweeping an arm around the perfect circle of stones. "I was chosen to bring this about. I channeled forces that terrified me with their enormous power. But the design was good; it could have held back the storm, perhaps, for eternity."

His voice broke, and he sat down. After a moment, Arni said, "Could have?"

Urkar's reply was flat and strained. "Those who wielded the destructive power fought us. Before our pillar was ready, they drew the storm toward it. Our structure had been built and the forces were flowing, but the strength of any pillar is in its core, and that—they shattered."

"Did the storm break, then?" Arni asked in awe.

"No; the pillar, this stone circle, endured. And even shattered as it was, the core still remained within it, adding slightly to its strength. But that has vanished now, because the core is gone. Once again a storm is building, sweeping this way, and now little remains to hold it back."

Jamie frowned as she tried to follow the story. This fellow, she tried to assure herself, was a madman—or, more likely, he and the rest of it were a nightmare. But neither lunatics nor nightmares let you go when you want out, so for the time being she might as well make what sense she could of this.

"But if you have that much power," she said, "you could repair the pillar thing, couldn't you?"

"No." He stared at each one, his eyes the color of Arctic ice. "But you could."

Chapter Six

Now Jamie knew this was a nightmare—or worse. Beside her, Arni was babbling about magic quests while Tyaak was going on about force fields and holographic projections.

Raking a hand through his mane of hair, the older boy said, "Even if I accepted this magic scenario, which I do not, I am the wrong person for your little game. I am a Kreeth, training to be a galactic navigator. I am—"

"Stubborn and blind!" Urkar cut in. "Have you never once seen something or done something which you could not explain with your crippled 'science'? Come now, the truth."

"No, never! Stellar navigation is an exact science. I could not possibly . . ." Tyaak slowed, then lapsed into a frightened-seeming silence.

Eyeing him curiously, Jamie spoke up. "Look, Mr. Urkar, you're wrong about me. The only thing I've ever wanted to do with the supernatural is to see ghosts. I don't want to *do* it. I don't want scary powers like that, and I don't have them! Whatever you need done, you'll just have to do it yourself."

"I can't!" he shouted. "Oh, all three of you are family, all right: as stubborn as they come. I'm not going to waste any more time with words. I'll show you!"

Urkar jumped to his feet and clapped his hands. Abruptly the fire snuffed itself out, leaving nothing but a glowing cloud of smoke. The cloud thickened and spread like dense mist. Slowly at first, then faster, it began to spin around them. Jamie felt Arni move beside her and grab her hand. Even Tyaak came a step or two closer.

Now the mist was spinning at such a dizzying rate, Jamie felt it draw the air from her lungs, the sight from her eyes, and even the thoughts from her mind. She wanted to scream but couldn't draw breath.

She had almost blacked out when the spinning suddenly stopped, throwing them all into a heap on the heathery ground.

Jamie opened her eyes to see Urkar struggling to free himself from the folds of his sealskin cape. He staggered to his feet. "Sorry, I think I got a little overhasty. Didn't gauge things right. But I haven't looked back here . . . in a long while."

"Where is . . ." Jamie started to say, but she fell silent. The utter stillness and the impossibly bright stars were gone. Overhead, a vast clear sky was tinged with approaching dawn. A steady sea breeze tangled her hair and carried with it the crying of gulls and a sound that might be distant song.

She looked around. They were still standing in a complete stone circle, but rather than seeming ideal and eternal, the stones looked raw, as if newly hauled from the earth and not yet worn by wind and rain.

Stretching off on all sides, the moorland seemed unbroken by roads or fields or even houses. On the lochs, not a single boat could be seen, only swans and white-fringed waves.

The singing voices were louder now, and Jamie could see a procession of people, clad in browns and grays, wending their way toward the circle. She stepped back into the shadow of a stone, but Urkar shook his head.

"No need. They can't see or hear us. This is the day of the circle's consecration. For an entire summer, the people of the island labored to build it. I selected the stones and determined their placement, and the others dragged them here and raised them while I fashioned the core. From the one grove of trees on the island, I chose three saplings. Then, with all the power I had, I fashioned them into three staffs embodying the forces of life—of air and earth and water. With spells and incantations, I wove the three into one, a single staff ending in three finials: a leaping fish, a soaring hawk, and the arched head of a horse. There, you can see it now."

Jamie and the others looked closely at the procession. Its head had already reached the deep newly dug ditch surrounding the circle. In the lead was a man wearing a sealskin cape—a short man with curly black hair and beard tinged with gray. Jamie gasped. It was Urkar.

This other Urkar held a wooden staff. Its shaft was

twisted and braided, and at the top were three carved figures.

Singing a clear rhythmic chant, the procession crossed the earthen causeway and entered the circle. As they did, some glanced to where the four watchers stood, but they clearly saw nothing except stone and heather. It's like being a wraith, Jamie thought with a shudder. Beside her, Arni jumped and waved his arms about, delighting in invisibility, until Urkar hissed, "Be still and watch."

Now the people were forming a circle within the circle of stone. Alone in its center stood the visible Urkar. As he raised the staff to the pale lavender sky, a chink of gold glinted on the rim of the eastern hills. Slowly the sun rose higher, and so did the chanting voices. The waiting stones turned from gray to gold.

The invisible Urkar turned to his companions. His voice was dry and bitter.

"Looks peaceful, doesn't it? A happy sacred ceremony completing this great work. Ha! That's how it would seem to those without the power to see more. But I did have the power, and so do you. Try. Look beyond this flat picture to the creative forces straining to connect with these stones and to those other forces seeking to destroy that tie. It's all there."

He began to hum a sharp piercing note that sliced into Jamie's mind and set her thoughts vibrating with it. The scene in front of her seemed to thin. The more she concentrated, the thinner it became, until the figures seemed nothing but faded paper cutouts against a background that was darkening by the second.

Black clouds were boiling over the horizon, rushing

forward with speed greater than the wind's. The seething edges were rimmed with pale green lightning. The three children shrank against the stones, but the crowd of people seemed totally unaware of what was bearing down upon them.

"What's happening?" Arni whispered.

Urkar's voice was harsh. "The forces of destruction trying to prevent this work of creation. They were too strong, too swift. Watch."

The man holding the staff looked uneasily over his shoulder at something those around him couldn't see; then he raised his voice in a new, urgent chant. The stones in the circle began to glow, not with sunrise but with inner power. Brighter and brighter they grew, until they became giant crystals of light. Then, like a fountain, their radiance shot upward, columns of light piercing toward the stars.

Inside the circle, the people took no notice even of this, though the man in the center again looked behind him and changed the speed of his chant. Raising the staff against the swirling, dark sky, he brought it down sharply, driving its point into the earth. The staff, too, began to glow, and thin tendrils of light began spreading from it over the ground toward the ring of stones.

Then came the thunder: a cataclysmic explosion that shook earth, sky, and sea and set the stones tottering. At last the people seemed to notice something. They scanned the sky to see if a distant storm was coming.

Like a vengeful spear, lightning struck, a bolt of vivid green shooting from the mountainous blackness. It pierced the glowing staff and, in an explosion of light, burst it apart. The cry of its bearer was lost under a final concussion of thunder.

When Jamie's sight recovered from the blast, she again saw the summer morning. But now the people were crying and wailing, picking themselves up from the ground and staring in horror at what lay before them. Their leader was sprawled, a charred heap in the heather. Nearby, three smoldering gashes showed where the sundered parts of his staff had burned their way into the earth.

A girl with raven-black hair gave a pained cry and ran forward to kneel by the body. But all life had been burned from it.

Jamie realized she was clutching both Arni and Tyaak. Instead of pulling away, she looked in wonder at the man beside her. His lined face was damp with tears.

"Uthna, my daughter. She, too, had the power, and it is through her that, in time, it came to you. But I had clouded her sight that day. I spared her from seeing the threat that was gathering and the danger in that final ceremony."

Abruptly he looked away from the scene and stared over the moors. His whole body was trembling, and Jamie almost wanted to put an arm around him.

Struggling to control his voice, Urkar continued. "They buried me that day, there in the center of the circle. The three pieces of the staff were left where they had fallen, hidden beneath the quickly healing heather."

"Then—the evil won?" Arni said, aghast.

Urkar shook his head. "No, not entirely, not then. The creative magic was weakened, but the shattered staff still remained within the circle, adding some of its power to that of the stones.

"And, of course, I was there, too. My task had never been completed, so I remained to watch over this pillar of life, to help it hold back any looming storm.

"For centuries I succeeded. Within the circle, my power remained strong enough to thwart any threat from magic or from evil intent. But time was at work too. Stones toppled; some were hauled off; and, far worse, one by one the three buried staffs were found and removed. No magic was involved, simply ignorance and chance, so I was powerless to stop it."

"Couldn't you just go get them back?" Arni asked.

Urkar gave a frustrated sigh. "No, there is nothing much left of me except power, and even that is strongest in this circle. I can leave its bounds, but only in some other, weaker form." Abruptly he turned back to face them. "But you three are alive. You have physical bodies of your own, and you carry a power as great as mine."

Arni smiled broadly. "So *we* are going to bring back the three sticks?"

"Yes."

Tyaak shook his head, violently sweeping the air with his dark crested mane. "What if we do not choose to go?"

Urkar spun upon him. "Choose? Did I choose to devote my life, not to family and friends, but to building a massive circle of power? Did I choose to die for it? Did I, a person with all the patience of boiling water, choose to spend eternity guarding that circle? No! I did not choose the power I was born with or the time I was born into—and neither did you. Of all my descendants, only you unlikely three happen to be alive at the right times to have even a hope of retrieving the staffs. You are untaught, yes, but together you may have enough raw power to manage it. But don't mistake me. It is not a choice I am giving you. It is an assignment."

Tyaak continued to argue, but Jamie had stopped listening. Suddenly a trembling smile spread over her face, and she burst in, "You're a ghost, aren't you?"

"What? A ghost? Nonsense, I have better things to do than mope around haunting people."

"But you died. I saw it."

"Of course I died. At some point in the stream of time, every one of you has died."

"Don't try to hide it in science fiction gibberish," Jamie said firmly. "You died, but you're still around. So you're a ghost."

Urkar gave an exasperated snort. "You are impossible! Look, will it make you happier somehow, having me be a ghost?"

Jamie smiled evenly. "All my life I just wanted to prove that I could see a ghost if one was around. If I've finally won that one, I might be willing to take on a little something more."

Urkar tore at his hair in annoyance. "All right, all right! I'm a ghost. Boo! Now, can we get on with it?"

Chapter Seven

When the gray mist swirled them away, it was at a more leisurely pace than before. Fighting dizziness, Jamie tried to concentrate on the instructions Urkar was giving them, but it was harder and harder to follow the words. His voice became a distant blur blending into a steady roar. The roar of wind.

She was lying on the heather within a broken stone circle. It was daytime, cold and wet. Jamie pulled herself up.

"Right," she said aloud. "I hit my head and have been having majorly weird dreams all night. I'd better get back before my folks call the police."

She strode off toward the road, then staggered to a halt. At the same moment she'd noticed that the road wasn't paved, that not as many stones were toppled as ought to be, and that she was wearing leather boots and a coarsely woven blue dress that hung below her knees.

"No!" She spun around. Her two young companions were still there. Arni was wearing what he had been, but now Tyaak was in a similar outfit. The half-Kreeth angrily threw back the wool hood from his bristling hair and glared about.

"Where is Urkar? Gone! Well, that lunatic may have dumped us here—whenever 'here' is—but I do not choose to stay. I do not choose to be part of this whole bizarre species!"

On behalf of humanity, Jamie objected. "Well, we certainly aren't any more bizarre than you, with your skin the color of swamp water and your hair like a half-shaved porcupine. None of us chose this, like Urkar said. What we've got to do now is figure out how to get out of it."

"That's simple," Arni said brightly. "All we have to do is find the missing staffs, and we're free."

Tyaak looked at him skeptically. "All right, Mr. Apprentice Wizard, do you know where they are?"

The boy's smile faded. "No, but magic should be able to help us."

"And you have some idea how to work magic?" Jamie asked.

Miserably Arni shook his head. "I wish Urkar had told us more. I always thought I had the power, but with the new religion around, no one dares teach it. I'm naturally good at finding things, but I don't know if that's magic or simply figuring out the sort of place something is likely to be. I don't know if I've ever actually worked magic."

He looked as if he were trying not to cry. Jamie stepped over and said, "That's okay, I don't either. My attempts were always busts . . . or crazy imagination."

Then she looked at Tyaak. "What about you? When Urkar asked if you'd ever done anything odd, you clammed up."

"If I did, it is my business." He looked away, then abruptly turned back. "But there is something very odd about this whole thing."

Jamie smirked. "Really? Just one thing?"

His eyes narrowed. "Either you are very stupid or you are part of a plot. How are we able to speak to each other? Urkar claims that he is from the Neolithic period, maybe six thousand years before my time, you two are from around the eleventh and twentieth centuries while I'm from the twenty-sixth. But languages change; people spread through time like that could not possibly understand each other. So this must either be a colossal hoax set up to fool me or—"

"Or it must be magic," Arni put in. "If magic can put you two into sensible clothes instead of those outlandish things you had on, then why can't it make you speak my language? Someone who goes around acting as superior as you ought to be able to figure that out."

"Now look, brat . . ."

Jamie stepped between them. "Hey, like it or not, we're stuck with each other here. Let's try to find those staffs and get this over with. Arni, since this seems to be your world, have you any ideas where we should start?"

"Birsay, I guess. That's where I'm from and where

Earl Thorfinn lives when he's not off raiding or fighting other Vikings."

Tyaak was staring off into the distance. "Well, perhaps those horsemen can give us a ride to this Birsay of yours."

Arni spun around, clutching the dagger hanging at his side. "Sure, unless they're enemies." Quickly he looked back at his companions and the short daggers on their own belts. "Swords against daggers. No good. We're better off if they don't notice us." He sprinted to hide behind a stone.

Before Jamie could follow him, she realized it was too late. The three horsemen coming over the moors had veered toward them and picked up speed. Jamie pelted past the stones, scrambled through the ditch, and took off at a run toward a large grassy hillock. A burial mound, she remembered from the tourist placard, and if it was open like that one on the hillside, she might be able to hide inside.

The air filled with yelling voices and the muffled thud of horse hooves. Jamie skidded around the mound, only to find it covered with unbroken glass. A shadow darkened the ground, and an arm reached down and hauled her roughly onto the back of a horse.

"Got one!" the man clutching her yelled. "Is that the lot?"

As Jamie struggled, the arm tightened and a coarse greasy beard scratched the back of her neck. One whiff confirmed that she was no longer in an age of mouthwash and deodorant.

"Let me go!" she heard Arni yell. "I'm Arni Arnorson. My father is Earl Thorfinn's skald. He—"

"—would be missing a son," a deep voice interrupted, "if we'd been supporters of the late Earl Rogenvald instead of followers of Thorfinn, his killer. But have no fear, Arni Arnorson, your red hair marks you halfway across the island. We were only having a bit of fun. Besides, you and your friends ought to stay clear of this circle. You know what the priests think of these places."

Arni snorted. "Well, priests don't know anything. And I am a person of power, a descendant of Eithne the Sorceress, so no one had better meddle with me."

The man laughed. "Oh, excuse me, most powerful Arni Arnorson. Will you use magic to waft back to Birsay, or would you accept a ride?"

Arni's voice shrank a little. "A ride would be appreciated."

The man laughed again. "And who are these other two, then? I don't recall seeing them about."

Arni looked to where Jamie and Tyaak were each seated in front of another rider. "Uh, no. . . . The girl is the daughter of a trader from Caithness. And the boy . . . uh, he is a slave sent as a gift to Earl Thorfinn by someone he met on his pilgrimage to Rome."

If she hadn't been so uncomfortable herself, Jamie would have laughed at Tyaak's expression. She wondered if Kreeth tended to bite. This one certainly looked as if he could.

The man holding the alien boy looked him over critically. "They do say there are odd-looking folk south of here. I'll not doubt them anymore."

The others nodded, impressed, while Tyaak looked angry enough to explode. "Well, enough dallying," the leader said. "The Earl needs to hear our news. It's not likely that Rogenvald's followers will attack before spring, but a warning will give Thorfinn the whole winter to prepare."

They jolted across the heather to a narrow dirt road. Jamie had always liked riding, though she wasn't a horse fanatic like some of her friends, but this shaggy beast's jarring gait did not make for a delightful ride, especially not when she was crushed between the animal's neck and a large smelly Viking. And the overwhelming fear and strangeness didn't help either.

The moorland looked more tended than it had in that brief glimpse they'd had of Urkar's time. There were well-marked fields and pastures, and an occasional huddle of stone houses. But this was also clearly not the Orkney on which she'd just been vacationing, with its paved roads and television antennas. The salt wind whipping at her face tore away Jamie's last shred of hope that this was a dream. In its place sat a hollow chilling fear. This was real, and it was up to three clueless kids to get out of it.

So maybe she'd better start with a crash course in current events. Trying to sound as casual as possible on this jolting horse, she said, "So, tell me more about this news you're bringing."

The man snorted. "Some wool merchant's brat wants to be part of state councils? Well, no matter, the word will be out soon enough. King Harald of Norway is out to avenge the death of his Orkney ally, Earl Rogenvald. He's promised men, ships, and arms to Rogenvald's followers to move against Earl Thorfinn. So when the seas warm in the spring, any of you merchants still around may find yourselves in the midst of a grand battle."

Jamie frowned, wishing she had read a bit more of those guidebooks. Who *were* those people? Well, it probably didn't matter, as long as they could find that wretched stick and get out of here—soon.

Their road threaded through the moor, crested a hill, and swept down toward the sea. Fields and houses clustered more thickly near the shore; beyond a stretch of choppy gray water, a wedge-shaped island tilted out of the sea. More buildings clustered on its lower, landward side.

The wind was stronger here and whipped the horse's mane into Jamie's face. Heading north of the mainland village, they stopped on a low cliff opposite the island. She and the other two passengers were swung roughly to the ground.

"You're on your own from here, O great Arni Arnorson," the leader of the men said. "Now just you remember this kindness when you set about casting evil spells." Laughing, the men guided their horses down a steep path to the beach.

Without getting too close to the cliff's edge, Jamie watched them. "Where are they going?" she asked Arni.

"Just down to the beach. The tide's nearly far enough out to cross over."

She studied the narrow channel of gray water between the shore and the island. Along a straight strip, it was churned into white foam with occasional rocks bereaking the surface. "You mean when the tide's out, that's not an island?"

The red-haired boy nodded. "For several hours at low tide, you can walk across at just this one spot. That's what makes it such a good defensible stronghold for the Earl. No one can easily attack by land."

Taking shelter from the wind behind a grassy hillock, the three waited and watched the spine of exposed rock gradually widen. The first to break the silence was Tyaak.

"Was it necessary to tell them I was a slave?" he asked crossly.

Arni shrugged. "Better than telling them you were from another world. The priests might end up by calling you a demon. Besides, not many of us have seen people from these southern countries."

Jamie tucked her woolen cape more closely around her. "I'd think your talk of working magic could cause just as much trouble with the priests."

Arni scuffed a foot in the sandy soil. "Maybe I shouldn't have said that. But they didn't even believe me." He gave the ground an angry kick. "And why should they? I can't really work it anyway!"

"Well, we'd better start trying," Jamie said, "or two of us are going to get stuck in a world where we don't belong."

"Then it is hopeless," Tyaak said flatly.

"No, it's not!" she objected. "We must be able to work magic. Urkar already had us doing it, looking through the sky to see that supernatural storm. I don't quite know how I did that, but I just kept looking harder and harder, like Urkar said, and then it was like I had switched on an extra battery or something because suddenly I *could* see deeper, and that made me want to look deeper yet."

"That's it!" Arni said excitedly. "I don't know what a battery is, but for me it was like discovering I had an extra arm or eye that let me do things I normally couldn't. What about you, Tyaak?"

"What about me what? This whole thing is ridiculous."

"But you saw through the sky, too, didn't you?" Arni demanded.

"Yes, but—"

Jamie interrupted. "So you tapped into some magical force. And you've done it before, haven't you? You just don't want to admit it."

"Nonsense! That had nothing to do with magic!"

"So what is 'that,' anyway?"

"Nothing! Look, the riders are starting across now. If we are going to do this, we had better go."

He headed quickly down the path and the others followed. Jamie didn't call Tyaak on the sudden way he'd changed the subject. She was concentrating too hard on hugging the inside of the cliff path. It had been safe enough for horses, she knew, but she always felt queasy on slanting paths with nothing along one side.

Once at the bottom, she decided to drop the earlier matter. Some things were best not probed at, she thought uneasily, and quickly turned to Arni. "Are you sure this staff is on the island?"

He shrugged. "Not *sure*, no. But don't you sort of get a feeling it is?"

Tyaak grunted. "The only thing you're feeling is that you have a home and food over there. But we have to look someplace." He walked to where the small beach joined the still-damp rocks and began to cross.

Sighing, Jamie followed. At the moment, food seemed as good a motive as any.

Foam-fringed ocean was still drawing away on both sides, but ahead of them now stretched a natural causeway of dark rock, water-worn slabs all tilting up at the same angle. The pattern was echoed in the cliffs of the island ahead, where slab upon tilted slab was piled up and capped with a layer of pale winter grass. The low end of the island that they were approaching seemed weighed down with stone houses, but the rest, tilting swiftly upward like the prow of a ship, was dotted only with white sheep.

But Jamie couldn't afford much sightseeing. The rocks they were crossing were damp and slippery. Several times her leather boots skidded into trapped pools of tidal water, sending tiny creatures scurrying out of her way. Once she reached down and scooped up a handful of little shells, pink, green, and white, and let them tinkle in her hand. But then she had to scatter them back. The heavy wool outfit she was wearing had no pockets.

The wind roaring through the channel was even noisier here. But once they stood under the island's dark cliffs, its song mingled with voices and barking dogs: the sounds of the village that began above them on the cliff's edge.

"The first thing we should do," Arni said as he stopped to wring water out of the hem of his cape, "is go to my house and get something to eat. Then we can plan our attack."

"What do you have in mind?" Jamie asked.

"Well, think. If someone were to bring home an interesting old piece of carved wood, what would he do with it?"

"Use it to start a fire?" Tyaak suggested.

"No! Wood's too rare to use for that. We burn peat. He'd probably use it as a walking stick or as part of a fancy piece of furniture. Or maybe as a rafter. Yes, I think that's it. Something high, near a roof, feels right. Come on. We'll eat first and then go around looking at all the rafter ends in the village."

As they climbed the steep path and then continued up the village's central street, Jamie realized that this would not be easy. All the buildings had stone walls with roofs made from slabs of grassy earth held up by beams, the ends of which just poked out from under the turf. A lot of those ends were carved.

But it was hard to look at beam ends with all those interesting people on the street. They were dressed in heavy woolens and various types of fur. On the whole, Jamie didn't think they looked either as mean or as clean as she'd imagined Vikings would look. Some greeted Arni as he passed, and gave his companions curious stares. She noticed Tyaak pulling his hood more tightly over his head.

"This is my house," Arni said proudly. Jamie was not impressed and, by the wrinkling of Tyaak's nose, she guessed that he wasn't either. She hoped that whatever code of politeness the Kreeth had would at least keep him quiet.

Pushing aside a leather hanging, they stepped through the low doorway. Inside, the rectangular stone house was all one room. Along one wall ran a built-in stone bench with bedrolls of blankets and furs. Most of the light came from the hearth in the center of the floor and from the smoke hole in the roof above it. Leather curtains were pegged firmly over narrow windows.

"Looks like Mother's out, and Father's sure to be with the Earl." Arni added proudly, "He's not only Thorfinn's skald, you know, he's also his cousin and friend."

At the moment, Jamie was more interested in whatever was in the iron pot that stood on a tripod over the fire. At the first whiff, she'd realized how ravenously hungry she was. Trying to warm up, they crouched by the glowing coals while Arni ladled a steaming mass into three clay bowls. Jamie cautiously poked at hers with a carved bone spoon. Some sort of mush with chunks of something else in it. Fish? Gross, she thought, but hungrily spooned in mouthfuls anyway.

After a couple of helpings, Jamie put down her bowl and asked, "This great-grandmother of yours, was she really a sorceress?"

"Oh, yes. But surely even in your times, you know the story of Eithne and the magic banner."

"Surely we do not," Tyaak grumbled, "and surely we do not want to, either."

"But you should anyway," the younger boy insisted. "After all, she seems to be your ancestor too."

Arni put down his bowl and sat up rather stiffly. His voice became high as he switched into singsong chant. "Now, after Earl Ljot's death, his brother Hlodvir took charge of the earldom and ruled well. He married Eithne the Sorceress, daughter of King Kjarval of Ireland and his Orkney bride, and their son was Sigurd the Stout. After Hlodvir's death, Sigurd became a great chieftain and ruled Caithness as well as Orkney, defending them against the Scots. Every summer he went on splendid Viking expeditions as well, plundering in the Hebrides, Scotland, and Ireland.

"One summer it happened that a Scottish earl challenged Sigurd to a fight and, as his mother, Eithne, was a sorceress, he consulted her, saying that the odds against him were heavy.

" 'Had I thought you wanted a safe life,' she taunted him, 'I would have raised you in my wool basket. But fate, not wiles, will rule your life. Take this banner. I have made it for you with all the skills I have. It will bring victory to the man it is carried before, but death to the one who carries it.'

"The Earl took the banner, finely worked with the figure of a raven. He gathered what men he could for the battle and sailed to meet the Scottish earl. The moment the two sides clashed, Sigurd's standard-bearer was struck dead. The Earl told another man to pick up the banner, but before long he too had been killed. In the end, Earl Sigurd lost three banner carriers but won the day.

"Five years later, Sigurd's allies in Ireland called on his help against King Brian. Sigurd came to Ireland with many long ships, but when the armies met, no one would carry the raven banner, so the Earl had to do it himself. And as his mother had foreseen, he was killed.

"Now, after the death of Sigurd—"

"Enough!" Tyaak said. "No more confusing names

and impossible coincidences. It is a stupid, unlikely story anyway."

Arni seemed to droop a little; then he stuck out his lip stubbornly. "It is a fine story. Maybe I didn't tell it as well as my father does, but I'm still learning."

Jamie shot Tyaak a dirty look, then assured Arni, "No, you told it very well. It's just that we'd heard all we needed to know. But I bet no one would carry the banner after that."

"They certainly wouldn't. It still hangs in Earl Thorfinn's hall, and his armies carry a different banner into battle." The boy shot a defiant glance at Tyaak. "I can take you to see it if you don't believe me."

"I believe that the same banner hangs there. What I do not believe is that it is magic."

Jamie smiled wickedly. "Well, if you don't believe in magic, how do you explain sitting here centuries before you were born?"

Tyaak shrugged. "Urkar possesses very powerful technology, whatever he chooses to call it. But he sent us here to find a particular object. And if we do not find it and bring it to him, he has no reason to use that technology to send us back."

Before, Jamie had shunted that thought aside, but now it wrapped her with the coldness of Orkney's wind. Clutching her cape more tightly, she whispered, "So we might have to stay on this bleak eleventh-century island forever?"

Tyaak nodded, and Jamie thought he didn't look as arrogant as before. He looked scared—about as scared as she felt.

Chapter Eight

T his is a fine place!" Arni had begun to protest,
when a dark figure stepped through the door.

"Arni! You've been gone a whole day longer
than your message said. Where have you been?"

"Mother!" Arni jumped up. "I, uh . . . I went to
gather roots for Isgard the Healer on the mainland and
got cut off by the tide. I stayed with these good people,
and they came over here to return the visit. But we've
got to go now and deliver the roots. I'll be back."

Quickly he hustled the others to their feet and out
the door, past his exasperated-looking mother. "Follow
me," he whispered. "Isgard's house is on the upper edge
of town. Might as well start checking roof beams there."

Jamie felt like an idiot, walking from house to house
looking under each roof like some eleventh-century
housing inspector. She'd have thought more people
would object, but all the concern and conversation she

picked up were about the news the riders had brought earlier.

Finally her fingers were so cold, she asked for a break from beam inspection, and for some information. "Look, Arni, have I got this anywhere near right? King Harald of somewhere . . ."

"Norway."

"Right. King Harald of Norway is paying a bunch of people to attack your Earl Thorfinn because Thorfinn killed another earl named Rogenvald. Right?"

The boy nodded. "Right, except that the paid fighters are joining former followers of Rogenvald who want to avenge his death. Last year Thorfinn surrounded a house where Rogenvald was staying and burned it down. Then he disguised his own ship with Rogenvald's shields so he could sail into the enemy's harbor and jump out and kill more of his people."

"Sounds pretty sneaky to me. Maybe your Thorfinn deserves to have people after his head."

Arni looked shocked. "But Thorfinn only attacked Rogenvald for revenge because before that Rogenvald had set fire to a house where Thorfinn and his wife were staying and they only escaped by leaping through a second-story window and rowing across the Pentland Firth at night."

Jamie shook her head. "Oh, and I suppose that Rogenvald only did that to avenge something else which—"

"Young Arni," said a deep voice behind them, "you are telling the story backward, but the gist's right. Soon you should have it in proper skald fashion like your father here."

The man looking down at them was huge and not the least bit handsome. His nose was a great beak, and on either side dark eyes glinted under shaggy eyebrows. His wild black hair was tufted here and there with gray. Altogether he was not a person to be ignored.

"Earl Thorfinn!" Arni exclaimed, bobbing his head. "My friends here are . . . not locals. I thought they needed to know all about your great deeds."

"And so should everyone," the big man boomed, "in Orkney, Scotland, and beyond." He bent toward them and winked. "Particularly since we are about to add a new verse. Come, all three of you must join us in the great hall tonight for feasting, drinking, and storytelling. Then your friends will have more stories worth spreading when they return home."

He straightened up and slapped the man beside him on the shoulder. The little gray-haired man staggered but kept smiling as if he were used to it. The Earl continued: "Even dead, that little weasel Rogenvald keeps pestering me. But come this spring, we'll finally put him and his minions to rest, and you, Arnor, and your son, too, can sing about it. In the meantime, though, we might as well enjoy ourselves!"

With a huge bark of a laugh, the Earl strode down the road. Arnor looked at his red-haired son, then cast a questioning glance at his two companions.

"Friends of mine from the mainland," Arni sputtered.

The skald squinted more closely under Tyaak's hood. "And from a bit farther away, too, I suspect. But the Earl has invited all three of you. Come early enough to get a place." With one more glance at his son's friends, he hurried after the Earl of Orkney.

Arni whistled with relief. "I don't know how long I'm going to be able to juggle these stories about you."

"Then let us find that stick and get out of here," Tyaak said impatiently. "Should we not be looking more in that direction?"

"Why that way?"

"It just seems— Because we have not as yet."

"Those are the big official buildings down there— the church and the Earl's residence." Arni puffed up a little. "As the skald's son, I see quite a lot of those places, and I've never noticed any carved beam end like the one we want."

Jamie tried to pull her cloak even closer; the sun seemed near setting, and it was getting very cold. "I still think it's stupid to look only for roof beams. It could be a soup stirrer or a fence post or—"

"No, it's high up. My magic tells me that much. Yours would talk to you, too, if you'd only listen."

Tyaak snorted, and Jamie kept silence. She supposed she'd be willing to listen if there were only something to hear. But all she had was a vague picture in her mind of what the staff should look like. Urkar hadn't even told them which of the carvings was here, but she imagined it was a bird—a black bird. That was just a wild guess, though.

"All right," Arni said, "let's head Tyaak's way. The Earl's feast will be starting soon, and we can check out the beams in the church on our way."

At the gate of the churchyard, however, they ran into Sven Havardson and several other boys.

"Well, if it isn't the failed swordsman turned sorcerer," Sven said wryly. "Worked any great spells lately?" Then he looked at Arni's male companion. "Would this be a demon you've conjured, and are taking to meet the priests?"

Hand dropping automatically to his dagger, Arni squeaked, "No! He's a merchant's son from . . . Constantinople." He turned to Jamie and Tyaak. "Come, we don't want to be late to the feast, not after the Earl himself invited the three of us."

He started hurrying down the road, then stopped and looked back at the group by the gate. "I've given up on the idea of magic—a waste of time. But if I did learn, I wouldn't bother conjuring demons, I'd start by turning the lot of you into something that suits you better—sea slugs, maybe."

With a confident stride, Arni continued down the road. "Pretty good," he muttered to Jamie and Tyaak. "I put them off the scent and put them in their place at the same time. Knowing I've got magic is almost as good as knowing how to work it."

They came to the Earl's hall. Again, Jamie was not impressed. All the stuff she'd read about medieval times had certainly glamorized things. At the moment, though, any place out of the cold and ceaseless wind looked good.

The building did have a wooden door, though—pretty impressive, Jamie admitted, for a place that hardly had any trees. Once they stepped through, the heat hit her numbed face like a volley of needles. Blinking, she looked around. The room was hardly a grand cavernous hall. It was built a lot like Arni's house, except for being several times longer and wider, but the thick stone walls with narrow shuttered windows looked the same. Built-stone benches along both walls were already filling up with guests, mostly men but a few women. They all had long hair, worn either braided or loose.

Arni led them to the back of the hall. The air was thick with smoke—and with smell. The pungent tang of peat smoke mixed with smoking grease from the pig roasting in the central fire pit, and to this was added the locker-room odor of crowded bodies that weren't bathed often. Jamie decided that the good thing about being cold here was that your nose couldn't smell much. Beside her, she noticed Tyaak pull his cape in front of his face and mutter something about "reeking Humans."

They settled into a corner of the far wall where they could see the length of the hall without being in the way. On either side were other rooms, curtained off. As they watched, the room filled with people. Their laughing, chattering voices swirled into the thick eye-stinging smoke, which was having difficulty finding its way out the hole in the roof. Women moved back and forth among the guests, pouring drinks from fat pottery jars.

Suddenly the curtain to their left was thrust aside, and Earl Thorfinn strode into the room, followed by his skald. Room was made for them on the benches, and the drinking and loud talking began in earnest. After a while someone called for a song, and a young man with a harp began a raucous piece that Jamie suspected she wouldn't have been allowed to listen to back home. Then there was a call for a story, and Arnor began chanting a tale about some ancient earl who apparently died when he scratched his leg on the poisoned tooth of an enemy whose severed head he had tied to his saddle. Gross, Jamie decided, glad she couldn't catch all the words in these singsong chants.

Instead of trying, she began looking around the long smoky room. Battered round shields hung on the walls, each painted with a different design. High above the door on the far wall hung a banner, a red background with a black raven. She caught her breath. This must be the magic banner Arni had told them about.

Was it really magic? Jamie tried to look at it the way Urkar had showed them, to look past the surface to the real thing. It did seem to be moving, like a bird flying into a sunset sky. But that could just be an effect of the rising heat and smoke.

Just looking at it made her feel tingly, though she could be making that up because she knew it was supposed to be magic. Still, there had to be *something* to this magic stuff, no matter what Tyaak thought. He just didn't want to admit that humans could do anything special.

Jamie looked over at Tyaak. Leaning against a door jamb, he was fast asleep. Now that he wasn't scowling and his porcupine hair was hidden under the hood, he wasn't really bad-looking—if you could ignore the old-avocado color. She ought to be angry at him for caring so little about human culture that he fell asleep here, but she was getting groggy herself. This whole weird day had been cold and exhausting. She was glad someone had started carving the roast pig, though it would be a while before any was passed their way.

Arnor seemed to have switched to a new tale, but the monotonous rhythm was the same. Something about two guys named Brusi and Einar who seemed to spend a lot of time fighting each other. She couldn't keep them straight, and it was too much trouble trying. It was too much trouble even keeping her eyes open in the warm smoky air. She let them close and let the skald's voice wash over her in warm meaningless waves. Wash into silence.

In the distance, a bird screamed. A raven. No, a person. Several people.

"An attack!"

"Rogenvald's men!"

"Sound the alarm!"

Chapter Nine

J amie's eyes flew open as screams and shouts erupted around her. Shields and weapons were yanked off walls. With a ferocious yell, Earl Thorfinn, wielding a huge ax, barged out the front door; others shoved and pushed to follow him. A few leaped over the crouching children and headed for other exits.

"Let's get out too!" Arni yelled over the clamor as he thrust aside a door curtain. "They might set fire to the place!"

"No!" Jamie shouted, pointing back at the raven banner. Suddenly she was seeing it for the first time, *really* seeing it. It pulsed — not with heat but with power. Power flowed through it like steady waves of flame. But even that was not what froze her to the spot.

It was the black wooden pole from which the banner hung. Like a long black serpent, it twisted with power of its own, older, deeper power, and the bird carved at its head seemed to unfurl its wings. Its beak opened in a silent scream.

"The staff!" Jamie cried, grabbing the other two. "There! The banner's hanging from it. We've got to get it!"

The hall was nearly empty now, but one of Thorfinn's men suddenly stumbled back through the doorway, another warrior raining sword blows on his upraised shield. Gripping his battle-ax, the first man fought back. Beyond them, the street was lit with tongues of flame.

Ignoring it all, Jamie raced toward the raven staff. Jumping on a stone bench at the end of the room, she tried to leap for a rafter. Just out of reach. Tyaak jumped up beside her, roughly grabbing her around the waist and boosting her to his shoulders.

Teetering precariously, Jamie clutched a rafter with one hand and with the other reached toward the banner. Still it was out of reach—inches away. She could almost feel its smooth wooden shaft fitting into her palm. She stretched farther, her fingers tingling with strain.

The whole banner shuddered and broke loose from the wall. Like iron to a magnet, the shaft flew to Jamie's outstretched hand. Her palm burned with its cool dark power as she fearfully clenched her fingers around it.

As Tyaak lowered her to the bench, several more warriors burst into the hall, stepping over the body of one of the earlier fighters.

"It's here!" a dark, bearded man yelled. "The magic banner. What a trophy!"

A taller man with a long blond mustache looked straight at Jamie. "There! Take it from them!"

The darker man ran forward. Jamie shrank back, and Arni jumped up beside her. Brandishing his dagger like a sword, he whispered to her, "Don't fight while you're holding the banner! Remember the curse."

The man grabbed for the dangling cloth, and Jamie let him wrench the whole thing from her. Her hand burned with its loss.

Another warrior charged through the door and came at the blond warrior, who ducked and brought his own sword up under the new man's shield. With a cry, the newcomer fell to his knees, slumping forward into a spreading pool of blood.

"Hurry!" the blond man yelled at his companion. "We've got what we want."

Just then another man burst in, saw his dead fellow, and with a yell of rage threw a spear. The banner-carrier took it full in the chest and toppled over like a felled tree.

In an instant, Arni leaped down and tore the prize from the dead man's hand. The blond warrior rushed at him. Quickly Arni jerked the banner from its shaft and flung the cloth in the man's face.

Clutching the staff, Arni dashed toward a back door. As Jamie followed, she saw the mustached blond tear the banner away just in time to meet sword on sword with the warrior who'd thrown the spear.

Arni led them through a maze of rooms toward another open door. Just as they neared it, a torch was hurled through, catching a pile of straw bedding on fire. Escape was cut off.

"A window!" Tyaak yelled. He fumbled with a shutter, then, breaking through, led the others out.

The street was full of people yelling, running, and fighting. Several buildings were on fire, and smoke billowed in blinding clouds through the air. Jamie had absolutely no idea where they were. Arni, too, stood undecided, then headed up the street where the fighting seemed lightest.

"No!" Tyaak yelled. "This way! Follow me!"

Midnight-blue hair streaming behind him, he charged past a couple of Vikings swinging axes at each other. Arni looked at Jamie, shrugged, and followed. Just as Jamie passed the warriors, she heard an ax crash into a skull. If there was a scream, it was lost in the general noise.

Tyaak turned a corner, then abruptly dodged down a narrow alley between two houses. The alley opened onto a lower street. There were fewer people about. A woman carrying a crying child ran past them, and a goat galloped out of another street, chased by a cursing man with a rope.

Without a pause, Tyaak darted across the street and into another alley. Just then, a voice behind them cried, "There! Get them. Get it!"

Jamie saw several men running down the street toward them. Their leader was the tall Viking with the long blond mustache.

"We don't have—" she started to yell. Then her eyes locked with his. Cold, dark eyes. And she knew they *did* have what he wanted.

Like a hunted deer, she turned and dashed after her

companions, yelling, "They're after us—after the staff! They know what it is!"

Ahead of them, part of a burning building peeled off and collapsed into the street, blocking the way. Arni started to turn right at an alley, but Tyaak yanked him left. They rushed down the narrow lane, only to skid to a halt: It opened onto the edge of a cliff. The only light came from the burning village and a cold scrap of moon glimpsed through wind-shredded clouds. But the dark emptiness in front of them was as unmistakable as the crashing of waves below.

Grabbing at a stone wall behind her, Jamie fought a wave of dizziness, trying to think calmly. They'd gone too far to be above the causeway here. But that wouldn't matter anyway, since the tide must be in now.

That didn't seem to bother Tyaak. He turned and trotted down a path sketched along the cliff's edge. Arni followed, clutching the staff like a spear. When Jamie heard the hoarse cries behind her, she followed as well, keeping her eyes on her feet and away from the dark, yawning drop beside her.

A glint of light caught her eye; she looked up to see a torch bobbing up the path below them. A torch and several figures. Beyond them, dark against the dark sea, was the slim outline of a ship. This must be the spot where the raiders had landed, defying Viking tradition and the winter sea.

The three fleeing children slowed and stopped. They were trapped. "The sea is the only way now!" Tyaak yelled over the wind. Unfastening his heavy cloak, he let it drop and leaped off the cliff. With a wild Viking yell, Arni did the same.

Jamie watched them vanish into the sucking, boom-
ing dark. Voices were coming at her from above, lights
from below. Fearfully she remembered the eyes of the
blond raider, eyes that opened onto power, dark destructive power.

Fumbling with the clasp of her own cloak, she
shrugged it from her shoulders. If she had to die ten
centuries before she was born, she'd rather go in a
clean, natural way like drowning.

She sprang from the cliff, and for a moment fear was
gone. All the world was wind and glimmering moonlight. Then came the cold concussion. She slammed
against water harder and colder than iron, then sank
into directionless darkness. Currents pulled at her, tum-
bling her over, spinning her around. They left her no
sense of direction, no clue as to which way was up—and
escape.

She was going to die. There was no fear now, just
anger. She was going to die for some failed hereditary
duty, while her closest family would never know how
or why.

Out of the darkness, something grabbed her. Some
horrid sea thing, but she hardly cared. It pulled her, and
waves of air broke over her face. Gasping through the
spume, she drew in deep breaths. The thing that had
grabbed her was a hand, Tyaak's hand. His hair floated
like inky seaweed around his dark face.

She tried to ask about Arni, but then didn't have to.
In the moonlight she could see his darkened red head
bobbing not far away. Clutched in his hand, the black
staff glowed like a water serpent.

"Swim," Tyaak urged them. "Swim to the main island." Jamie, still confused in the darkness, had no idea where that was, but the Kreeth boy kept tugging her in one direction until she quit treading water and moved into a regular swimming stroke.

It was cold. Soon she could barely feel her arms and legs moving. Then, through the surging whitecaps and the tangle of her own hair, Jamie made out a black cliff looming closer and closer.

Rocks smashed against her feet. She tried to stand, but the waves rolled her over, throwing her against the shore. Her hands tore at sand and rock, trying to hold on. Slowly she dragged herself upward. Other arms reached for her, pulling her into the knife-cold air. Several stumbling steps, and she was huddled in the sand beside the other two.

For a long minute, all they could do was shiver. Then Arni said, "Got to get off the beach, head for the circle. If some of those raiders weren't just avenging Rogenvald but were after this staff, they might not give up."

Remembering the blond raider, Jamie forced herself to her feet. Weakly they scrambled to the top of the cliff. Once free of its shelter, they were hit by new volleys of wind that cut like steel through their dripping clothes.

Pushing through the gusts, they stumbled over dry, flattened grass. There were no trees or rocks, just open rolling land—open to the wind, to the night sky, and to any eyes that might be seeking them.

The raiders had boats. If they believed they could still lay hands on the staff, they could row over here, Jamie thought, and hunt the three of them. They could even steal horses from a farm and ride them down. She had to hurry, hurry.

Her legs had almost stopped obeying. They buckled at nearly every step, and the wind was rising. It was a struggle just to stand against it.

"Here," Tyaak's voice called. "Some sort of shelter. We can rest here. Arni thinks a storm is coming."

Low, broken stone walls. An old shed or something, Jamie thought as they staggered into it. In the back enough roof was left to hold off some of the wind and the rain that was now flying with it like tiny spears.

The three huddled together, listening to the raging night. At least this rain should put out the fires in the village, Jamie thought. Poor Arni. He was probably worried sick about his family and friends. At least hers were safe, even if centuries away. She reached around Arni's shoulder and found Tyaak's arm already there. They shivered together.

"Arni, Jamie," Tyaak said after a while. "Can either of you, uh, do that thing Urkar did with fire?"

"Start a fire by magic?" Arni whispered. Then, with renewed spunk, he added: "Suddenly you believe in magic?"

"Of course not. But somehow Urkar was able to make a fire back there, and we could certainly use one here."

"But he said some magic words," Arni protested, "and I don't know any."

"Maybe we can use the staff," Jamie suggested. "It's magic."

Tyaak snorted. "Oh indeed. Just say, 'Stick, give us

a bonfire—and some roast meat, while you are at it.' Sorry, it was a stupid idea."

"No," Jamie said, "the idea's great. It's just that we don't know how to use the staff. But, hey, Arni, you were right about the staff being high up, close to the roof."

"It was you who saw it."

Jamie was silent a moment. "Yes, and when I did, it looked exactly as I'd imagined it would. Maybe I hadn't just imagined it. Maybe I'd *known* what it would look like."

Tyaak just grunted. Briefly Jamie thought about what had happened afterwards—about yearning for the staff and feeling it shoot toward her. She shied away from the memory and quickly spoke to Tyaak.

"Well, at least you were right about the part of the village where we should be looking." After a thoughtful moment she added, "In fact, not only did you sort of lead us there, you led us through the fire and the streets and even the water afterward. Aren't you kind of *unusually* good at that?"

Tyaak said nothing.

Jamie looked toward his huddled shape. "That's it, isn't it? You've felt your power before and it was something like that."

"I do not want to talk about it."

"You'd better, though. You probably saved our lives."

After a long pause, Tyaak said gruffly, "I had been training as a navigator. I was good at it. My father said so, everyone did. But it is a complex skill. Some people are good at languages, others have a way with engines — I just had a knack for the mathematics and instrumentation used in navigation. Then once, on a training mission, our little ship developed a core disphasing, and most of our systems were damaged. It was up to me to navigate back to the nearest base. It was difficult with some of the equipment out, but I did it. We survived. It was only afterward that I discovered that our entire navigation system had been out. I had done it totally . . . on instinct."

"So, did you tell anyone?" Jamie asked.

"No! It terrified me. No one should have been able to do that. I was afraid it was some primitive, demeaning Human skill I had inherited from my mother. I didn't want anyone to know."

"Well, now you know you needn't worry," Arni said. "Most normal humans couldn't do it either."

"Why not shut up," Tyaak snapped, "and do something about a fire."

"Won't," Arni said, crossing his arms.

Jamie was too cold to be stubborn. She picked up the staff and poked its tip into the grass at her feet. "Look, let's all three hold this thing and think about fire. Then at least we can imagine being warm."

Jamie didn't know what the others were thinking about, but she imagined the fires they sometimes had in the family room. Her parents would be reading; her brother would be studying, stretched out on the floor with the cat on his back. The picture made her achingly homesick, so she switched to a summer campfire. Blazing at first, so you had to keep turning yourself like meat on a spit, one side to the flames, the other to the cold dark pine woods. Then dropping to dancing yellow flames in which you could see dragons, dancers, and fantastic cities. Finally came the coals, glowing embers like newborn jewels, perfect for roasting marshmallows and stretching toes toward to soak up the last of the warmth.

She could almost feel it again, warming the tips of her toes and slowly spreading its healing warmth upward. She sighed and opened her eyes, and still the embers glowed at her, smug and fierce like the eyes of dragons.

"We did it," Arni whispered.

"How?" Tyaak said, but no one gave an answer.

The fire grew from embers to a small patch of cheerily dancing flames. The lack of fuel didn't seem to bother it at all.

"You know," Jamie said after a time, "we should be giving some thought to this. Is it us, is it the staff, or is it both? If we can . . ."

Her words dried up. In the stormy darkness beyond their shelter, there was something darker. A shape moved toward them.

Their fire glinted in its eyes.

Chapter Ten

Staring in terror at the thing, Jamie slowly realized it was not one of the Viking raiders. It was a horse, a shaggy gray horse. Her eyes flicked to its back, but it carried no rider.

The horse, however, was staring just as hard at her. Its eyes in the firelight were bright blue. With a snort, it took several steps closer and roughly butted each of them with its head. Then it nudged the staff at their feet.

Arni jumped up. "It's him! Urkar's a horse!"

"Ridiculous!" Tyaak said.

"Why?" Jamie asked, thinking about blue-eyed sheep and owls. "He said that outside the circle nearly the only thing he had power to do was change shapes. And look at the eyes."

"It's an animal. A blue-eyed animal."

Standing up, Jamie tentatively patted the horse's

neck. "All right, but it's just the kind of animal we need to get out of here before anyone tracks us down."

"But there are three of us," Tyaak pointed out.

The horse turned and trotted off into the rain and wind. Jamie was about to snap that now they didn't even have one horse, when they heard several whinnies and saw their horse returning, herding two others as if it were a sheepdog.

Arni was jumping about like an excited flea. "He's rounded up two farm horses for us. I get the gray!" Grabbing the staff, he burst out of their little shelter and swung onto the blue-eyed horse's back.

The shaggy brown horse nearest Jamie did not seem very happy to be there. It stood with head down and legs braced against the wind. Jamie guessed the gray horse had gotten it there with a little mind control and a lot of bullying. She patted its shoulder. It shivered but stayed still. Stepping onto a broken stone wall, she clambered awkwardly from it to the horse's back.

The blue-eyed gray nudged and nipped the remaining horse, a black mare, over to another wall so a reluctant Tyaak could do the same. "I cannot believe how primitive this is," he muttered once he was mounted. "Using animals for transportation."

Jamie snapped, "So maybe you'd rather walk all the way back to the stone circle with sword-swinging Vikings at your heels?"

The gray horse nickered, stepped over to their fire, and deliberately crushed it out with one hoof. Then it gave the other horses swift nips, and they were off.

Once they were fully clear of the sheltering ruins, the rain and wind hit like a club. Jamie flattened herself against her horse's neck, surprised that the animal could even stand up in this, let alone see where it was going. The sheets of rain were so thick, she could scarcely glimpse the horses ahead.

After seemingly endless riding, she noticed that the rain, if not the wind, was slackening. Then, as if they'd stepped through a curtain, the rain stopped and the howling wind tore apart the clouds that had covered the moon. By its chill light, Jamie could see they were following a narrow mud-slick road cutting through grass and heather. She strained to see ahead and caught the glint of moonlight on two stretches of water.

The horses moved steadily on; Jamie clung to hers for warmth as much as for safety. She was sorry she no longer had her cloak. It would be just as soaked as her other clothes, but still it would be one more layer against the wind. Her fingers were too cold even to feel the coarse mane she was clutching. She wondered how long it took for someone to die of exposure.

A cry pierced the wind. A bird, Jamie guessed, but what would a bird be doing out on a night like this? The cry came again, clearly from behind. Awkwardly, Jamie turned to look.

Riders. Four of them, coming fast. One called again, and she knew it was not a friendly hello. It was a Viking war cry like the ones she'd heard during the raid.

The gray horse jolted into high speed and the others followed his lead, making their riders clutch frantically to stay on.

Jamie peered ahead through her horse's flying mane. Yes, she could see it—the stone circle. Not far now. But their pursuers were not far, either.

The ditch encircling the stones, stretched like a shadow across the ground ahead. Suddenly Tyaak's horse stumbled and the boy went flying into the heather. Horrified, Jamie looked behind. The riders had nearly caught up with them. If they didn't know who was carrying the staff, they might go for Tyaak. She yanked at her horse's mane, trying to make it turn, but it charged straight ahead until it met the gray horse charging back.

One Viking had already dismounted and was running with upraised ax toward the fallen boy. Tyaak struggled to his feet and tried to dodge, but the gray horse, with Arni clinging to its back, galloped past him, reared, and brought hooves down on the startled warrior. Through the screaming wind, Jamie heard a cry and a muffled thud as the man toppled to the ground.

Jamie saw another rider bearing down on them. She kicked her horse and it shot off willingly, but in the wrong direction. Yanking at its mane, she tried to turn it toward the stone circle. The other rider was close behind her now, but cutting toward them came the gray horse.

Jamie tugged at her horse again, and it turned so suddenly she found herself slipping from its bare back and flying onto the heather-carpeted ground. Not very softly carpeted, she thought as she lay breathless, looking up at the racing moonlit clouds.

The Viking reached her. Coldly he looked down from his horse, his eyes like pools of darkness. It was the mustached blond from the island. Then his attention snapped toward Arni, who was barreling toward them, yelling and brandishing the staff over his head. Jamie saw the man's face light up. He had seen what he sought.

The blond warrior raised his own cry, drew his sword, and drove his horse toward Arni's. The little gray veered away, but not soon enough. The sword swept down toward the boy and all he could do was raise the thin wooden staff to ward off the blow.

Steel met wood in an explosion of light. Fire ran down the staff to the sword and ignited the warrior as if he were a fuel-soaked rag. His horse reared in terror and threw the flaming man to the ground.

Jamie staggered to her feet, then turned away, trying not to be sick. Nearby, Tyaak was trying, too, and failing.

Then Jamie remembered the other two warriors. Like dark shadows, they were closing in. Arni, still clinging to the gray horse, feebly shook the now darkened staff at them. They halted. Jamie and Tyaak both took this chance to run for the stone circle. They were close now, and with every stride they were coming closer. Jamie heard hooves but didn't dare turn. Just think about feet, she told herself, feet pounding over heather and moon-pale grass.

The ditch. Down it and up again. Through the circle of stones, Tyaak just ahead of her. She turned. Arni and the gray reached the ditch and leaped it. Behind them, the two riders were about to follow.

Then they were gone. No, Jamie realized, they were probably still there, leaping over the ditch. It was their quarry that was gone. As the mists swirled and spun, Jamie sank shakily to the ground. She had never been so happy to be miserably dizzy in her life.

The mist cleared to show the changeless stones and the high, crystalline stars. The silence was so deep it almost hurt her ears. Jamie looked around her. Arni and Tyaak were nearby; but in place of the horse, Urkar stood in the center of the circle, black staff in hand. He raised it point downward and jabbed it into the earth.

Jamie cringed against an expected explosion. But the earth only trembled slightly and was still.

As though reading her thoughts, Urkar turned their way. "It's just one staff. I need three to do anything worth doing."

"It did pretty well back there," Arni said quietly.

"Correction: *You* did pretty well. The staff has its own little ways, but it was your power it fed on."

"*I* did that?" Arni gasped. "I cremated that man?"

"With a little channeling from the staff. But don't fret. If he had guessed the kind of threat you posed, he would have tried something of the same on you. He had the power, that one, though it came from the other source."

With a casual pass of his hand, Urkar started a small campfire. "But never mind all that. You succeeded. And quite frankly, I wasn't at all sure that you would, family or not. Come, warm up a moment."

Suddenly the flames twisted flat as a rush of wind howled through the circle. Spinning around, Urkar raised his arms and yelled something into the sky. The wind faltered and died away.

"The storm!" he explained angrily to the huddled children. "It's drawing closer. I can't stop time, for all that I can move within it. At its front end, time is still moving forward, and that is where the storm will break. You must be off after the second staff."

Even Tyaak could only groan in protest, but now his groan was one of three.

Urkar sighed. "Mortals! You need to rest and recover. Get over here by the fire, then."

Willingly Jamie did so, slumping into an exhausted heap on the heather. The heat of the fire seemed to reach into every fiber of her. She closed her eyes, nestling into a cocoon of healing warmth. Dimly she heard Urkar's voice ranting about patience. It seemed as distant as the stars.

Chapter Eleven

What woke her was change, like falling asleep in a steadily moving car and waking when it stops.

There was cold and the noise of wind, vast outdoor wind. Jamie rolled over on the crackly, pungent plants. She opened her eyes.

It was night. She sat up. A half moon lit up the broken stone circle and the white tourist placards.

Confused, Jamie sat on the cold ground, torn between delight and startling sadness. It *had* been a dream. She'd gone out to the stone circle to defy those petty signs. She'd fallen, hit her head, and had this long, incredibly real-seeming dream.

It was over. She was safe, and yet she felt she'd lost something precious. Even the idea of doing things supernatural instead of just seeing them wasn't all that bad. But that had been a dream, too. And it was a great relief to know she would not be lost in some dead time, pursued by terrifying powers. She was finally safe.

Or she would be as soon as she trotted back to their house, let herself in, and crawled into bed. Cautiously Jamie stood up, but the dizziness had gone. She took a few steps toward the road.

"So this is your world, is it?"

She almost screamed. Spinning around, Jamie stared into a dark greenish-brown face. Beside the alien boy, a smaller red-haired boy smiled excitedly. "A lot more stones have fallen. Do priests still tell you to stay away from here?"

Stunned, Jamie stammered, "No, just tourist signs. You're real."

"Believe me," Tyaak said sarcastically, "I am just as *delighted* to see that you are real, too. I had almost convinced myself that some native insect had bitten me and I was having a toxic hallucination."

"You two are awfully hard to convince," Arni said. "Magic is real. I guess it isn't always fun, but it *is* real." Jamie thought the boy sounded a little less enthusiastic than he had before, but she couldn't blame him. Before "magic" came into her life, the only killing she'd seen had been on TV.

Tyaak ran a hand through his hair, and Jamie noticed it wasn't nearly as bristly as earlier. It must have had some sort of treatment, which all the wind and rain had taken out. She would have felt smugly amused at the thought if she hadn't remembered the treatments she'd gone through herself to produce various hair looks. Anyway, she decided, Tyaak's almost limp hair fit in better with the jeans and jackets all three of them now seemed to be wearing.

"That Urkar person infuriates me," Tyaak said, giving his hair a few more futile fluffs. "He never once thanks us for risking our lives to retrieve his stick; then he gives us no choice about coming here, either. Suppose we refuse to do any more of this?"

A tempting idea, Jamie thought, trying not to recall that last onslaught of storm. "I suppose that'd be all right with me. This is my world, after all, and I could just go about my business. But if we quit now, I'm not sure how Urkar would feel about returning you two. You're right, he's not big on gratitude." With a sly smile, she added, "But maybe you'd come to love my Earth and fit right in."

Tyaak shot her what on any planet would have been a dirty look. "So where do you think this stick is on this precious world of yours?"

That shook her. She hadn't given it a thought. "How should I know? It's a big world. Some farmer could have picked it up for a fence post, or some tourist could have taken it halfway around the world as a souvenir."

Arni's eyes opened wide. "Halfway around the world? Do you think that's happened?"

"No," Jamie said firmly, then wasn't sure why. "I mean, I have no idea."

"Oh, but you do, I think," Tyaak said with an infuriating smile.

She glared at him. "All right, maybe I do have some sort of hunch that it's still on this island, or maybe I just hope that it is, so we don't have to go traipsing all over the world looking for a stupid stick. What about you, Mr. Navigator? What direction is it in?"

"I couldn't say."

"Yes, you could! East, west, south, north. Try, or you'll never get back to that fancy superior planet of yours."

He scowled at her, but closed his eyes and stood still for long moments. Then he opened his eyes, shrugged, and waved an arm to the northeast. "Perhaps that way, but just as likely not."

Jamie frowned. That didn't help much since from what she remembered of the map, much of the island was that way. She turned to Arni.

"And what about you? Any feel for whether it's up high or down low or anything?"

He didn't have to close his eyes. "I don't know about high or low, but there are people about. Lots of people."

"How many?" Jamie pressed. In his world, lots of people could mean a dozen.

"Lots and lots. And lots of . . . of space, too. No, maybe not space. Things that take up space."

"Like buildings?"

"Maybe," he said a little doubtfully. "Built things, anyway."

Jamie thought a moment. "Lots of people and buildings could mean a town, and there aren't many on the island except Kirkwall and what's-its-name, the port. Only Kirkwall's in that direction, though, so let's start there."

Tyaak was again trying to fluff up his hair. "Are you planning to walk, or do you have horses too?"

Jamie sniffed. "This century isn't the Dark Ages, you know. We have cars and buses."

"Gasoline-driven, I suppose? How primitive."

"Well, feel free to walk if you want. But we're not going anywhere just now, except back to my house." She thought a moment and asked, "Do you suppose it's the same time now as when I left here?"

"It was for me," Arni said. "I didn't lose any time at all in Urkar's circle. A great magic worker like him could probably put us down at any point of time he wants."

"Well, I hope so," Jamie said, starting off toward the gate. "Otherwise I'm going to have a lot of explaining to do—to my parents and probably the police."

"Police?" Arni questioned.

"People who enforce laws and look for missing people. Let's go."

Walking along the road, Jamie enjoyed the feel of paving underfoot. Arni apparently did too. He skipped on ahead. Then looking himself and the others over he said, "This is what you people wear? Girls, too?"

"Yes, and I like it that way. I don't miss that heavy itchy wool skirt one bit. But the jeans and jacket look great on you. You'll fit right in." She studied Tyaak. "You might, too, but you'll have to keep the jacket hood up over your hair." She wasn't as sure about Tyaak's complexion. He could be a tourist, maybe, who was perpetually seasick.

As she walked, Jamie realized that although she was sleepy, she wasn't as exhausted, wet, and bruised as she should have been. Urkar's fire was pretty good stuff. She was thinking about Urkar when she saw her house down the road and suddenly realized she couldn't just march in with two strange boys and hide them in a closet.

"Look, you two are going to have to wait outside somewhere until morning and then knock on the door, like we've arranged to have you visit or something. Maybe you're friends I've made on the island, and we've arranged to go to Kirkwall together."

"I have no desire to spend more time outside, thank you," Tyaak said. "Is it ever anything except cold and windy on this planet of yours?"

"Hey, don't judge the whole planet by the Orkney Islands," Jamie protested.

Arni piped up, "And don't you two run down Orkney. When my father and Thorfinn went to Rome they said the people and weather there were soft—it was just the sort of place that ought to be plundered. Orkney people are tough."

And stupid, too, Jamie thought, if they don't take the first chance they can to leave. But she kept quiet. Orkney was proving a more unusual vacation spot than Florida.

"There's a carriage house or something behind our place. It'll keep you out of the wind, and anyway it's supposed to be spring here."

Predictably, Tyaak didn't like his lodgings, but Jamie didn't really care. She was only as tired as if she'd been out half the night defying tourist signs, but that was tired enough. Her father was still snoring when she slipped back inside the house and climbed the stairs. To that rhythm and the steady roaring of wind outside, she fell into a deep, restful sleep.

When Jamie woke in the morning, wind was still riffling over the slate shingles. As she lay in bed, pictures fell into her mind, and she played with them like fragments of a dream. Only they didn't fade as the minutes passed, but became more clearly linked together.

All her life, she had wanted to be something special. Yet now, the knowledge that she *was* special seemed more frightening than her earlier fear of being a nothing. Being plain unremarkable Jamie might have been disappointing, but it wasn't terrifying.

But it wasn't exciting either. Now, both terrified and excited, she quickly got up and dressed.

A muffled knock downstairs. Moments later her mother came up, a slightly puzzled look on her face. "Jamie, there are a couple of boys at the door who say you arranged to go with them into Kirkwall."

"Oh, yes," Jamie said stepping onto the landing. "I met them yesterday when I was . . . exploring around and got talking, and we sort of decided it would be fun to go into town and look at the shops and stuff."

She hurried downstairs. Two boys stood in the dark entryway gazing around. The taller one had his hood pulled up to shadow his face, but one strand of hair had escaped like a blue-black snake.

"Mom," Jamie said awkwardly, pointing first to the red-haired boy, "this is Arni. He's a local resident. His father's a . . . writer. And this is Tyaak. He's, uh . . ." For a moment her imagination ran frighteningly dry. Then it burst free. "He's from Afghanistan. His family are, you know, refugees from that war they have there. They're thinking of opening a restaurant here."

"What a fine idea," her mother said. "And I'm sure you'll all have a grand time in Kirkwall. Now, if you boys want an extra breakfast, you can join Jamie. Her father and I ate early so we could get a good start on today's birding trip. Do you have any money for the bus, Jamie?"

"Yes, Mom, I'm fine. Say hi to the birds."

Jamie was relieved that her parents left before Arni and Tyaak did much at the breakfast table. Neither seemed to know how to deal with the food or utensils. Arni ended up eating the scrambled eggs with his fingers. After a few pokes, Tyaak wouldn't eat the eggs in any manner, but he did slice the banana lengthwise and roll it and the bacon in a piece of toast.

The bus proved even more of a challenge. Arni acted as if he'd rather attack the thing than ride in it, and once Jamie had managed to get them all up the steps, Tyaak insisted on standing behind the driver and asking what every control was and how it worked. After a while, the man glared around at him.

"You pretending you're a flipping bus inspector or something?"

Jamie dragged Tyaak and Arni to seats in the back, away from other passengers. Once Arni got over his distrust of the machine, he eagerly joined Tyaak in looking out the window and flooding Jamie with questions.

"How do you heat these big houses?" Arni asked, and before Jamie could explain about furnaces and fireplaces, Tyaak asked, "Are there still fish in the seas for people to catch and eat? I thought they nearly all died out in the twentieth century. Or maybe that was the twenty-first."

Great, Jamie thought. Now I'm a guide for time travelers—a new profession. Trying to keep the other passengers from hearing, she answered questions as well as she could. It surprised her to realize how much she didn't know about her own time. How did gasoline-driven engines actually work, anyway? And how many different religions were there in the world?

When they finally got to Kirkwall, Jamie was relieved that both boys were too busy looking even to talk. But once on the street, she had to deal with Arni's ignorance of traffic and Tyaak's tirades against primitive, carelessly piloted death traps.

In the shopping area set off for pedestrians only, she relaxed a little and asked, "Now what? Is this what you mean by a lot of people, Arni?"

He nodded solemnly. "This is more than a lot. But yes, I think it is right."

She turned to Tyaak, who was staring at a window full of puffin souvenirs. "And what about you? Any idea about direction?"

For a moment, his dark face clouded, and Jamie was afraid he was going to start denying again that he could do anything. Then he shrugged and said, "Up that way, perhaps. But I am not a calibrated homing device. It is just a vague pull, a feeling of rightness somehow. I could as easily be imagining the whole thing."

Jamie nodded. "Yeah, I know. I have a picture in my mind of this staff being pale, like sunlight glimmering on fish scales, like when a fish jumps out of the water. Every time I tell myself that's silly and try to think of it some other way, I keep coming back to a fish, a jumping fish. I just wish Urkar had taken the time to show us how to use this power, but I guess he's not a time-taking sort."

They headed up the shopping street, looking at window displays that were amazingly futuristic or crudely primitive, depending on the point of view. Jamie noticed the same local teens lounging about with the same tank tops and cool expressions, trying to look scornfully superior to the gawking tourists. She'd have liked to shove their smugness in their faces by telling them just how far from home *these* tourists were, but instead she traded impudent stare for impudent stare and walked on.

Soon the narrow street opened up, the shops continuing on one side and the plaza with its cathedral and cemetery on the other. "Are we still heading in the right direction?" Jamie asked.

"Yes," Tyaak said, then shook his head. "I am not certain. This is like trying to tune myself to a very narrow frequency and picking up many other signals instead. And I do not know how to adjust the scanner — assuming the principle works at all."

Arni looked confused, but shrugged and said, "The staff is around people and built things and space."

"And it's upright instead of horizontal like the last one," Jamie added. "But that still doesn't get us far. Look, if this power thing's too slippery, let's just use our heads. What we're looking for is a carved wooden staff, an old one. Now, someone who found something like that would probably keep it at home as a curiosity or give it to a museum or a college or something. I think there's a museum down that way, across from the cathedral, though I don't know what it has."

"What's a museum?" Arni asked.

"A place to keep old things that show about the past."

"That's silly," the Viking boy said. "If old things are any good, people should use them; if not, they should throw them out."

"Spoken like a barbarian," Tyaak said scornfully, heading down the street.

The museum was indeed full of old things: furniture, glass, and silver from the last few hundred years; jewelry and inscribed stone from Viking times; and bone, pots, and stone tools taken from ancient burial cairns. From the first, however, Jamie felt that the staff was not there. In fact, the place made her uneasy, and it seemed to do the same for the others, too, though they dutifully examined everything.

Three times, Arni went back to the Viking exhibit only to walk away quickly, looking even paler than usual. "Let's go," he said at last. "What should be here isn't, and a lot of things that shouldn't be here are." He hurried down the stairs and headed for the door.

When they reached the bottom of the stairs, Jamie said, "Wait, let's check out the gift shop."

"They sell antiquities?" Tyaak said, surprised.

"No, but they might sell carvings by local craftspeople or maybe have some guidebooks or something useful."

She led them into the little room, but after glancing around, she felt there was nothing there for them. In fact, this was someplace they positively did not want to be.

She was backing out when a young man stepped from a back room and asked, "May I help you?"

Jamie wanted to bolt but tried to smile politely. "No, just looking. Taking in the sights, you know." Then she added awkwardly, "Particularly the old things. Are there other museums around—or other places where there are old things for people to look at?"

The young man studied her closely, probably trying to place her accent, Jamie decided. He had thin brown hair and glasses, and his chin was wisped with what looked like an attempt at a beard. Maybe he was just nearsighted, but she didn't like his intense stare.

"What about the cathedral across the street?" Tyaak asked. "That should have many old things in it."

"It does," the young man said, quickly shifting his gaze. Tyaak just as quickly lowered his. "But you don't want to go there. That is to say, you can't. Unfortunately, the cathedral is closed this week for repairs. There are many antiquities on the island, though."

"Anything else in town?" Jamie asked.

"Well, there's the earl's palace."

"Earl? What earl?" Arni asked eagerly.

"Earl Patrick Stewart built it in 1607. He was a foreign tyrant and not much loved here, and the whole place fell to ruin after a hundred years. You leave here and turn right, then left at the end of the block. You'll want to look at the bishop's palace too; that's part of the complex. The first part was begun by Bishop William the Old in the twelfth century. Then, if you want farming history, there's the—"

"No thanks," Jamie said. "Those places sound fine. We'll just give them a look and be on our way."

She hurried out the door, through the front courtyard, and onto the sidewalk. Leaning against a building to catch her breath, she shook her head. "Definitely the wrong place. And I didn't like that guy one bit. Come on, those must be the ruined palaces over there."

As they started off, Tyaak looked across to the cathedral. "Too bad that place is closed. At least it's still intact. Those palaces look too ruined to hold an old stick."

When they arrived, it was clear he was right. The buildings were roofless, walls holding the stone traceries of empty windows to the sky. Between the ruined buildings, a grove of leafless trees rose up like huge claws. In their branches, a flock of black rooks cawed raucously at one another.

Discouraged, the three sat on a bench. "This isn't right," Arni said. "Plenty of space but no people."

Tyaak nodded his head so that another lock of hair slipped from his hood. In this light, Jamie thought, the green cast of his skin wasn't terribly obvious.

He scowled up at the trees. "All I pick up here is the racket of those wretched birds. Why would any civilized species allow such creatures to inhabit their towns? And do you realize how much this town smells? Of fuel and garbage and unwashed people as well as animals? It is almost as bad as that Viking place."

Jamie bristled but didn't bother defending Earth cities. They weren't as bad as all that, though they could be a little smelly at times. Those birds, though—they *were* obnoxious, and kind of creepy too. The sky had been blue, but now banners of gray were sweeping in

from the west. Against that, the skeletal trees and
hunched black birds looked like a Halloween card.

As she gazed up, one of the birds spread its wings
and dropped from a branch. It swept down and down,
directly toward them. Its cry was like a saw rasping
iron.

As the bird swooped over them, Jamie looked up.
Her frightened eyes met the rook's, eyes like no bird
ought to have. Eyes like flaming ice—glinting a bright
piercing blue.

Chapter Twelve

C rouched on the grass, the three of them watched
the bird. Cawing harshly, it glided over the street
and the cemetery wall. Then with an abrupt
flutter of black wings, it landed on a tombstone.

"Urkar again," Tyaak said with a disbelieving shake
of his head.

"Do you think we're supposed to look at that tombstone?" Arni asked. "I'm sure not going to dig up any
old graves, if that's what he wants."

Jamie stood up and continued staring toward the
cemetery. The rook sat there cawing and occasionally
flapping its wings. Just beyond his tombstone, the side
wall of the cathedral ended. Around the corner would
be the stone arches of the front doorways. People were
moving back and forth as if going in and out of a door.

"Hey," she said suddenly, "the cathedral's not
closed. People are using the door."

"But the man in the museum said . . ." Tyaak began.

"He could have been mistaken," Arni said doubtfully.

"Or he could have wanted *us* not to go there," Jamie said. "Which I think means we'd better—quick."

Dodging traffic, she crossed the street, with the others close behind. Marching across the plaza, they easily opened the wooden door set in a stone archway and stepped inside.

It was like stepping into a different world. Outside was full of busy daytime noises, but in here those were all shut out. There were people about, tourists, but they talked in whispers that rose into the arched spaces overhead, blending with the echoing footfalls from the tiled floor. Outside, the cold had been driven by a fitful wind, but in here the cold was deep and still, like water pooled at the bottom of an ancient well.

Jamie looked about, trying to stretch her senses and pick up any hint of power. But it was hard to sort out anything from a general feeling of awe. Massive pillars of red stone, like the trunks of huge trees, marched down the nave. At the cathedral's sides, they stretched into arches that crisscrossed high stone ceilings, but in the middle they supported two tiers of colonnades that rose even higher into the ribs of a great arching vault.

Jamie glanced at her two companions. Tyaak was looking around with interest, but Arni was standing stock still. No, not still. He was trembling.

"Arni, are you okay?" she asked.

"It's so big," the boy whispered. "I thought the church Earl Thorfinn built was grand. Who built this, I wonder?"

Jamie shook her head. "I don't know. Stuff in the museum said it was named after some old saint called Magnus, but I don't know who he was or anything. Maybe we should pick up a guidebook. It could help with the search, anyway."

She walked over to where a plump woman in a bulky pumpkin-colored sweater was selling guidebooks, postcards, and bookmarks. The woman looked up with a big gap-toothed smile, and the whole effect as so jack-o'-lantern-like that Jamie struggled not to laugh.

"Could I have a guidebook to the cathedral, please? Something that tells about its history and where things are, maybe."

"Certainly, ducks. It's this one you'll be wanting. Looking for anything in particular, are you?"

"No," Jamie said firmly. She did nòt like nosy bubbly people who called her "ducks." "We're just tourists seeing what there is to see."

"Well, there is a great deal to see here. Maybe too much for lively young people like you. You might want to spend your afternoon doing the shops instead."

"No, no," Jamie insisted. "This is very interesting, really. Of course, I'm sure the shops are too. We'll just take a quick look around here and then maybe try them."

With her guidebook purchased, Jamie walked away wondering if she was getting paranoid or if everyone was trying to keep them from looking around this cathedral.

"So what does it say about who built this place?" Arni asked once they'd settled into a couple of the plain

wooden chairs meant for worshipers to sit in when tourists weren't overrunning the building.

Jamie flipped through the book looking for the answer to Arni's question, though he kept wanting to stop
and examine each picture. Finally she said, "Looks like
it was begun in 1137 by Earl Rogenvald—not the same
one your Thorfinn fought. According to the chart, this
Rogenvald was Thorfinn's great-grandson. He named
the cathedral after his uncle Magnus, who was killed by
some cousin. That's how he got to be a saint. Anyway,
that was about a century after your time. It started out
as a smaller church and lots of people have added to it
since."

Arni reached over and shut the book. "No more. I
don't think I like this magic traveling."

Jamie looked at his face, so pale that the freckles
stood out like splattered paint. "But you get to . . ."

He shook his head. "I'm dead. They're all dead—
Earl Thorfinn, my parents, everybody I've ever known.
The oddments in a museum and a few sentences in a
book—that's all that's left. I don't even know what happened the night of the raid. Did my family survive? Did
the Earl?" He slumped down, looking very small in his
modern bright jacket. "I want to go back."

Jamie gave him an awkward hug. "So let's go find
the staff, and maybe that old wizard will let you go
back."

She pulled the young Viking to his feet and hurried
him over to where Tyaak was studying a stone slab
carved with a praying woman and a staring skull. "I do
not understand your culture," he said, "nor do I want
to. But some of this is pretty morbid."

"It is," Jamie agreed, "it's grisly. But don't blame *my* culture. This planet has a whole bunch of cultures. Now, let's start looking for the staff so they don't all get blown apart and so we can get home."

Tyaak nodded, shoving strands of bluish hair back under his hood. Then he pointed vaguely down the nave. "That way."

As they walked slowly along, Arni said, "There are people here, and lots of space, and constructions in the space. It feels right. What do you see, Jamie?"

"Just the same, the leaping fish. But . . . it's not alone. Someone is—"

Her eyes suddenly focused, not on her vision but on the view over Arni's shoulder. At the guidebook desk, the woman in orange was talking to the man from the museum.

Grabbing Arni and Tyaak by the shoulders, Jamie hustled them down a side aisle. "Hurry! We've got to find it *now*!"

The cathedral was full of nooks and crannies. Every stretch of reddish stone wall seemed to be carved with zigzags or figures of animals and plants. Carved tombstones were set into the walls, and there was plenty of carved wood as well—intricate screens, altars, doors, and statues. Each choir pew ended in a carved figure of angel or demon or animal. But there was no leaping fish.

Jamie was looking at things so intently, she was getting a headache. The gray light that had been sifting through the high windows was fading rapidly. Alarmed, she glanced up. Beyond the clear glass, the sky had turned slate gray. In the very back of the building, where stained glass soared to the high ceiling, all the vibrant blues and reds had turned dark and sullen.

Jamie began to feel urgency building like a storm, and, from the pace of the others, she could tell they felt it too. As she turned a corner, a tall man suddenly loomed over her in the fading light. A statue. A king holding an ax. Jamie wondered if he'd liked to fight with an ax or if he'd been martyred by an ax murderer.

"That's Saint Olaf," a cheery voice said suddenly. Jamie spun around to meet the jack-o'-lantern grin of the woman in orange. "The statue was presented to the cathedral in 1937 as a gift from the church of Norway. Charming, isn't it?"

"Uh, yeah. Nice."

"Sorry, ducks, it's nearly closing time. Won't you please head back this way?" She pointed down the aisle they had just worked their way up.

Jamie was surprised when Tyaak's dark hand clasped her shoulder. "Yes, we will go now, but by the way we have not seen yet."

Firmly he guided her to a monument-filled far corner where a marble man reclined on his tomb as if it were a living room couch. Urgently the three scanned the area while the orange woman tromped purposefully toward them.

Jamie deliberately moved away from her and, half running, almost collided with another standing statue. "Bishop William the Old," a neat white label said; if she hadn't been so frightened, Jamie would have laughed. Who would want to go down in history known as "the Old?" She glanced up at the carved face. It looked old all right, but also . . . familiar. She'd seen it, just as she had seen the fish arching itself into a crook at the top of his bishop's staff.

"A local carver made that one," the orange woman said right behind her.

"But the bishop's staff is of a much lighter wood," Jamie said mildly.

"Yes; supposedly the carver incorporated into it some old relic he'd found. Good thing you had a chance to see this statue. It's scheduled to be sent to Edinburgh tomorrow for some restoration work. But really, I must insist that you be on your way, children. It's past closing time."

Gripping Jamie's arm, the woman propelled her down the aisle. Desperately she glanced back, but the others had caught the message. Arni had climbed onto Tyaak's shoulders and was reaching to pull the staff from the statue's grip.

Jamie let herself be led meekly away. The only sounds were their echoing footsteps on the tiles and the rising thrum of wind against the high windows. Beyond, the black sky was lit by a sudden flash of lightning.

The crash that followed wasn't just thunder. It was the statue of William the Old toppling to the floor with two boys toppling after it.

With a shriek, the plump woman turned and lumbered back. Sprinting past her, Jamie glimpsed the museum man running along another aisle.

Jamie reached the fallen statue, gripped the carved fish, and pulled the staff loose as easily as a sword from a scabbard. Arni and Tyaak were already leaping up some stairs to a narrow iron-studded door marked Exit. They pulled the handle, but it didn't budge.

The woman had caught up and fiercely tried to wrench the staff away from Jamie. Tyaak butted into her bulk like a football player, sending her bouncing back against a wall. Jamie leaped over William the Old and dashed in front of the altar. The young museum man stood there, cutting her off from a far door.

"Stealing church property? Give it here, please."

"No!" Jamie cried, darting between the choir pews. As the man lunged for her, the air cracked explosively and turned white. Dazzled, Jamie stared toward the great window at the front end of the nave. The building shuddered with the thunder; then the window turned from lightning white to storm black.

Recovering, Jamie dodged around the pews and raced across the far aisle to another exit door. The two boys were there already, struggling to open it. Failing, they turned to run again, but both pursuers blocked them.

"All doors except the main one are locked at closing time, children," the man said smoothly. "Give that to me, and we'll let you out."

Angrily, Jamie turned back to the door. She jabbed the lock wildly with the point of the staff. "Open, blast you!" she yelled.

The flame that sprang from the staff was like a welding torch. The iron bands on the door turned white hot. With a screaming crack, the old oak planks split apart.

Chapter Thirteen

Jamie stood for a moment, staring dumbly at the smoldering staff in her hand. Then she charged through the shattered door, Tyaak and Arni right behind her.

Outside, the rain lashed down in a curtain the color of knife blades. They were in the cemetery, but could see only a few feet ahead of them. Tyaak took the lead. His hood blown back, dark hair streaked behind him as he dodged this way and that. The others followed, leaping graves and veering from tombstones that seemed to plunge at them through the rain.

Running through the cemetery gate and down the street, Jamie didn't need to turn to know those other two were running after them. She could feel the hatred they shot before them like headlights. And she was the little animal trying to get off the road.

The rain was too heavy to really see where they

were going, but splashing through torrents of water, she and Arni blindly followed Tyaak. Suddenly a bus showed in the murk ahead of them. This was the spot where they'd gotten off earlier. But the bus was already pulling out. They'd never make it.

The bus blared its horn and squealed to a halt. Sprinting even faster, Tyaak reached it and began pounding on the door. The driver hit his horn again, then opened the door. Panting and dripping, the three children clambered on. As Jamie was fumbling for her money, she glanced out the bus's front window. Through the blur of rain, she made out a cow. It stood in the center of the street, staring placidly up at them with large blue eyes. Then it turned and ambled out of the way.

Muttering something about rural routes, the driver gunned the engine and jolted them forward. Jamie thought she glimpsed two bedraggled figures standing in the street behind them and shaking their fists.

The three staggered to the back of the jouncing bus and dropped into seats. They shivered, letting water drip off them into spreading pools on the floor. For the first time, Jamie really looked at the staff she was gripping. At its top, the carved fish, still glistening with real water, seemed ready to leap free.

"Those people," Jamie said at last, "they must be the same sort as the Viking raiders who followed us."

Tyaak was wringing water from the long dark ropes of his hair. He grunted. "I wish Urkar had told us more. If these are the workers of destructive power he mentioned, are they as ignorant in all this as we are? Were they simply ordered to capture the banner or protect the staff, or do they really know what is going on—about the storm and everything?" Suddenly he slammed his fists together and almost snarled.

"What's the matter?" Jamie asked.

"I am talking as if I believed this garbage!"

Arni laughed for the first time in a long while. "What is there to believe? Magic happens like the sun rising in the morning."

Jamie was running her fingers along the smooth swirling grain of the staff. It felt warm and tingly. She wondered if anyone could feel that, or just carriers of power. "Those others must know more about some things than we do. I bet if they got their act together, they could do us some serious harm—magically, I mean."

"But we have the staff," Arni pointed out.

"Right," Jamie said. "But do we have any idea how to use it? What I did was an accident—instinct, maybe—and it was probably the same with you, Arni."

The boy looked down. "I was just trying to fend that fellow off as if I had a sword. I didn't guess . . ."

His voice faltered, and Tyaak stepped in. "That is the danger. We have a tool in our hands we do not know how to use. Magic, as you call it, is probably some rational understandable power like any other force in the universe. We just do not know the rules. And I, for one, am not interested in learning. The sooner we get this into Urkar's hands, the better."

Jamie had been watching through the rain-blurred windows. "Our stop is coming soon. It's a ways from the circle, and there's nothing to have kept those two from getting a car and following us. If they know as much as they seemed to, they might also know where we're going. The Viking raiders did."

All three stared out the fogged-up back window, wiping little clear patches. But the road behind looked empty. Just the same, when the bus jerked to a halt at their stop, they hurried down the steps and headed up the road at a trot.

The rain had lessened, but the wind seemed worse, driving the cold and wet into them like needles. They had passed the remains of the earlier circle and were crossing the causeway between lochs when something made Jamie look around. A red car was speeding along the road behind them.

"Run!" she yelled, and dashed along the wet pavement. At each side, waves crashed and foamed against the rocks. White forms huddled together on the most sheltered side: wild swans, waiting out the storm.

The land widened out. They could see the jagged gray stones on the moor ahead. Arni left the road and began running crosscountry toward them. Jamie and Tyaak followed.

Behind them, the car rumbled across the causeway and, in a slurry of mud, pulled off the road. Two people in raincoats jumped out and started running after them. From the shape of the slower one, Jamie knew there was an orange sweater under the raincoat.

The wet heather was hard to run through. It kept snagging her feet, grabbing like tiny prickly hands. With a gasp she saw that that was what they were: little clusters of dark brittle hands, reaching out for her, grasping her shoelaces, clutching her ankles. Yanking away from them, Jamie struggled on. Then, swifter than a snake, an arm from a taller bush hooked her about the knees and sent her sprawling.

Wet heather slapped her in the face. Staring into it, Jamie saw writhing hands inches away. With her free hand she battered them back and felt tiny nails ripping her skin.

She heard an animal yell beside her. Half sitting up, Tyaak was thrashing in the heather. The expression on his face, alien or not, was pure terror.

Just beyond him, Arni was kicking and stomping. Then, with a squeal, he threw his hands over his face and stopped moving.

"It's got to be magic!" he yelled. "They're making us see things that aren't there. It's just heather and grass!"

Sure, Jamie thought, heather and grass with tiny hands. But that was crazy! Plants couldn't have hands. It had to be some nasty illusion.

Even as she thought that, the vividness faded. The hands went pale and gray, feeble as spiderwebs.

With an angry laugh, she kicked free of them and leaped over to where Tyaak lay fighting with nothing. Grabbing his shoulders, she tried to drag him up. "Better believe in magic!" she yelled. "Or you'll never see that this *is* only magic."

He looked at her, confused. She thrust the staff into his hands. "Come on, you can see through this. You've got the power!"

Leaning on the staff, he struggled to his feet. Hesitantly he swept the staff through the heather. Those smoky little hands, which Jamie could still see, withered and vanished. Tyaak's triumphant yell was cut short by words slicing through the wind.

"Child's play. Congratulations, but that's as far as you go."

Nearby on the moor stood the two from the cathedral. They had stopped to see the effect of their trick, but now advanced again. And they were not alone. Beside them moved other dark figures. Deadly dark — except for the eyes.

Jamie turned to run, but other shadows were moving down the slope, shadows with eyes like glowing coals. "You're all illusions!" she shrieked. "You're not real!" They scarcely flickered. The things reeked of power stronger than illusion.

The three children banded together, looking fearfully at the closing figures. "The staff?" Tyaak said doubtfully.

Jamie grabbed it. Yelling like someone in a samurai movie, she ran up the slope, swinging the staff against the nearest figure. Its eyes flared when the staff sliced through it, and the whole creature burst into flame. But this was worse. Now a huge tower of flame advanced toward her. She swiped at another advancing figure and another. They too exploded into menacing flame.

Those two know how to use their power, Jamie thought despairingly, and we don't. She tried to see nothing but damp heather beneath empty gray sky. But she could feel the heat and see the heather beginning to smolder and smoke.

A hissing screech cut through the crackle of flame. White shapes dropped from the sky. Staggering, Jamie fell back into one of the flaming towers, but its heat was fading and she could see right through it.

Everywhere, white wings, necks, snapping beaks. Wild swans, dozens of them. They beat their wings and dove, hissing and biting, at the raincoat-clad figures. With angry cries, the two raised their arms to ward them off.

Jamie flinched as one swan peeled away and dove at the three of them. It beat its wings and struck like a snake, driving them up the slope, fleeing its fierce blue eyes.

Through fading flames and shadows the three ran toward the stones, real and solid, that rose in a broken circle out of the moor. Three children and a swan burst through.

Sobbing for breath, Jamie dropped into the heather. The ground was dry, and the sound of rain and wind had vanished. A dark man with the swan's blue eyes stood over her. Smiling weakly, she handed Urkar the staff. Then she rolled over and snuggled closer to the gently burning campfire. She wanted only to be warm, dry, and asleep.

Chapter Fourteen

W hat woke Jamie this time was the sound of wrongness. She opened her eyes and saw the perfect circle of stones still around her, still lit by the ruddy glow of the campfire. Above stretched the infinite darkness with its icicle glint of stars. But the perfect silence was gone. The roar of a distant storm shot her with fear.

Shivering, Jamie sat up. Nearby, the others were sitting as well, their eyes turned to the center of the circle. Urkar stood there beside a slender pillar, dark wood and golden twisting together, taller than either staff had been alone.

He walked toward the three of them. "I can't keep the storm away much longer. Once it breaks into this little island of eternity, there won't be much time before it sweeps into your world like a flood. For years destruction will rise in power, until this whole chunk of the universe collapses. The only thing that will hold it back is raising this completed pillar. Up now! You must seek the third staff."

"But Urkar," Arni said uncertainly, "the magic — there's so much of it, and it's so powerful. I don't want to go off again with tools I don't know how to use."

Urkar snorted. "Do you think I want to be stuck in this changeless nowhere, able to dip into real time only as some powerless animal? Do you think I want to send off clueless raw recruits on a mission this important? Do you think I want—"

Jamie burst in. "Stop shouting, Urkar! Can't you see that Arni is scared? We all are, but Arni's the only one who wanted this power in the first place. And all it's done for him is make him incinerate someone and send him to a time when everyone he knows and loves is dead. I feel sorry for your daughter, if this is the kind of explaining, patient parent you were."

Urkar's face boiled with anger, then slowly calmed to a sad smile. "And well you might feel for my daughter. She was just like you, putting me in my place when I needed it."

He squatted down beside them. "Look, Arni, your people weren't dead when you climbed into another century. They were just where and when you left them. Think of time as a tree, a huge one. It starts as a seedling and begins to sprout at the tip. Branches spring out; it grows taller and wider. The growth is still only at the tip, but the whole beautiful creation is still there, still alive.

"Time is like that. The growth is only at the front end, but the rest of it, where the growth used to be, remains. From my little island in eternity, I can see the whole thing, I can go to any part I want, from the trunk to the growing, fragile tip."

He stood up again and paced nervously around them. "And that is where you need to go now. Young Tyaak here comes from the time on the edge. I had despaired of success there. The staff had left the island; even in animal form, I cannot leave these shores. My descendants had long ago left as well. But then Tyaak returned, and perhaps now, with all three of you, unschooled as you are, working together it is not too late."

"But what can I—" Tyaak had begun when a sudden gust of wind howled past them, shaking the stones where they stood.

Urkar raised his arms and shouted something, but the roaring wind tore away his words. Across the arching sky, a tiny gash appeared, stretching by the moment. Blackness oozed from it, deep, infinite blackness blotting out the stars.

"Hurry!" Urkar shouted. "Time is running out!"

Jamie, Tyaak, and Arni grabbed each other as the dizzying mist slammed into them, throwing them to their knees. Jamie felt as if a lifetime of sickening carnival rides had condensed into a single moment. The mist cleared, leaving them gasping and retching on the heather.

"In rather a hurry, isn't he?" Arni said feebly.

Jamie nodded, surprised to find even that much of her body still working. "He has good cause, but he does kind of overdo things."

"Not that it will do much good," Tyaak said staggering to his feet, "since I have no idea where to find that staff. If it has been taken off the island in my time, it could be anywhere in the universe."

Wind was sweeping steadily over the moor, but overhead the sky was clear and sunny. Only a few stones of the circle still stood. Others looked like gray whales, their sides just breaking above the blooming heather.

Arni gazed around, then looked down at the coppery jumpsuits he and the others were wearing. "This is your time?" he said in wonder.

The half-Kreeth broke into a smile. "As if I had just left it a moment earlier."

To Jamie the land looked much as it had millennia earlier. Hardly any roads or buildings, no boats on the water or vapor trails overhead. Yet the stone circle itself was clearly far more collapsed. The twenty-sixth century? Suddenly she felt as coldly lost as Arni must have. She and everything she had ever known were dead. She didn't belong here.

Tyaak, however, happily threw back his head, his dark hair streaming loose on the breeze. "I am back, and all this might never have happened. I could walk over those hills, get in my ship, and go home."

As he took a few steps, Jamie jumped to her feet. "And not even look for the staff? And leave us stranded in this empty time of yours?"

He turned, a wry smile on his face that suddenly reminded Jamie of Urkar. "I said I *could*. Kreeth and Humans, it seems, may argue a lot, but we do not walk out on duty. Even if it is a duty we did not choose."

Arni smiled eagerly. "So, where do we look for it?"

Jamie could see Tyaak's calm suddenly evaporate.

She stepped in. "Well, if the staff has gone off the island, we'll have to go, too. I suppose you have some sort of spaceship parked around here?"

Tyaak nodded bleakly and pointed north. "We could walk, but if time is that short, I had better bring it here." He plucked a small device off his belt and looked at it a moment, seeming happy just to have these things with him again. Then he punched a couple of buttons and gazed northward.

In moments, a silver speck appeared above the horizon, moving swiftly toward them. Tyaak walked briskly out of the circle, but Arni, dropping a hand to a belt that held no sword, stayed with Jamie behind the line of fallen stones.

The speck became an oval and dropped smoothly toward the moor where Tyaak stood. Silently it settled onto the heather. Arni looked at Jamie, took a deep breath, and set off toward it.

Soon the young Viking was running his fingers over the ship's smooth silver surface. Then he joined Tyaak inside and began asking a steady stream of questions.

Jamie hesitated by the open door. Suddenly she didn't want to be a part of this. For Arni what he saw now was so removed from the world he knew that it wasn't like the future—it was like magic. But she had grown up expecting a future of spaceships and aliens. Now it was here, and her time undeniably was gone.

Relax, she told herself. Pretend this is a "Star Trek" episode. That got her through the door and into the dental-chair-like seat that Tyaak pointed to. Jamie lay down and closed her eyes. Panic still gibbered at her, but she fought it back. Relax, she told herself again.

This is happening and there's nothing you can do about it except find that staff, take it where it belongs, and go home.

Gradually she did relax; with a sigh she opened her eyes. Having a goal, she thought with a smile, certainly does help stubborn, goal-oriented people.

Tyaak had already closed the door and was sitting in front of a low bank of controls. "This is ridiculous. If this magic is real, I should be able to just feel the right direction to go look for that staff."

"So, can you?" Jamie asked.

"That is the ridiculous part," he said in a small voice. "I think I can. It makes no sense, but I know where we should be heading."

"Then let's do it!" Arni said.

Another moment's silence; then Tyaak sat forward and adjusted some controls. Soundlessly they were rising over the island. Jamie stared into the view screen in front of her seat, safely removed from any sense of height. Purple heather, gray-green grass, dark ocean meeting the coastline in lacy white waves. Where maps in her time had shown the town of Kirkwall, there were still some buildings. The large reddish one might have been the cathedral. Then there was ocean, a few more islands, more ocean, and another coastline. More purple and green, with a few roads and clustered buildings. Scotland?

"Are we headed south?" she asked.

"It seems so. I set the coordinates by . . . instinct. Frightening."

They flew on, passing over more empty land. If this was Scotland and England they were flying over, Jamie thought, there ought to be more cities. She and her parents had passed through a lot on their drive north. But Tyaak looked so drawn and tense, she didn't want to ask him anything more.

Instead, Jamie played with the controls on the screen in front of her. She could change the focus, zoom in for closeups, or switch the view to the back or sides or even straight up into high deep blue. She walked over to show Arni how to do the same with his. He was so excited by the whole thing he could hardly sit still.

Then there was a city ahead. Not huge, perhaps, but a real city, a cluster of sun-glittering buildings along a river.

"This is it," Tyaak said. "The third staff is down there somewhere."

"Where is this?" Jamie asked.

Tyaak read off his screen. "A native town, capital of a former nation-state, name: London."

"London?" Jamie peered at her screen. Surely it had looked bigger a few days ago when she flew in to it. A few days ago? She shook herself and tried to focus on business.

"Arni, can you sense anything about the staff here?"

His brow furrowed under the thatch of red hair. "It's high. Not as high as we are now, but high. And there are a lot of strange things with it."

Jamie sighed. That wasn't much help. A lot of "things" in twenty-sixth-century London would seem strange to a Viking.

"What about you?" Arni asked in return.

Jamie was surprised. She hadn't given it a thought, but now she could see the staff clearly. "It's the horse carving, of course, the only one left. But the wood is very pale, pale as bone." She jerked back. She was sure of something more. "There are hands holding it, green hands. Pale green, like celery."

"Celery I do not know," Tyaak said, "but *pale* green would not be Kreeth, it would be Valgrindol. Not many Valgrindol on this planet, I should think."

"Not many people at all, by the looks of it," Jamie commented, scarcely wanting to ask the next question. "Why? I thought the historical trend was for populations and cities to keep growing."

"On Earth?" Tyaak said scornfully. "Humans had pretty well used up the planet when the Kreeth and others arrived. Most were eager to leave the place and settle elsewhere. That is what my mother's ancestors did. The planet is coming back, though. The oceans, land, and air have been cleaned up, and much of the plant and animal life is returning. But most Humans have set roots elsewhere. The ones here now are mostly hermit types or academics or people promoting tourism. There is not much trade, though, that a backward, used-up planet like this can offer."

Jamie decided all that didn't bear thinking about just now. Instead, she watched the screen as they dropped toward a field pocked with oval, round, or triangular craters of different sizes.

Tyaak was continuing his own thoughts. "That is what puzzles me. Valgrindol are largely traders—high-class ones. What would one be doing here on Earth?"

The movement of the ship was so smooth that Jamie could tell they had landed only because the view on her screen was stationary. Arni was still playing with his controls, scanning the city on one side and green fields and woods on the other. He zoomed in on the tall gleaming buildings towering into the afternoon sky.

"We're going out there?" he asked in awe.

"Yes, in a minute," Tyaak replied. "But I cannot go out looking like this." He walked to a section of wall and pressed something; a hood projected outward. He stood under it, and the long blue-black hair now falling in a flat mane down his neck was suddenly pulled up and out in a spiky crest. Then the hood retreated. Jamie and Arni just stared for a moment, then burst out laughing.

"You look," Jamie said between gasps, "like an electrified hedgehog."

"And here you were just starting to look normal," Arni said wiping his eyes.

Tyaak sniffed indignantly. "*Now* I look normal. Like a normal Kreeth—or close enough, anyway. A full Kreeth's hair grows this way naturally, but I have to work at it. Now, if you are through showing how provincial you are, let us go."

Opening the door, he led them out. They weren't in the open, as Jamie had thought. Transparent roofing ran between the landing craters. Some of these dimples held huge ships, blocks and blocks long. Others held vessels whose sizes ranged from a jumbo jet to that of a small compact car. Most were empty.

"How do we get out of here?" Arni said, looking over the vast field and its maze of ships.

"On one of these." Tyaak walked to a corral holding various sizes of large tall boxes. All were silvery on the bottom half and clear on the top.

"We have no luggage or goods, so a smaller transport will do." He looked at his companions and shook his head. "And I doubt you are up to driving individual models."

They climbed into what looked like a large shower stall with several rows of seats. Tyaak sat behind the controls and soon had them gliding off. "Sorry if I'm slow," he muttered tensely. "I am not used to navigating by instinct."

Jamie didn't want to disturb him, but one question wouldn't go away. "I didn't see wheels. How do these things move?"

Tyaak shot her a superior, pitying glance that she would have liked to slap off his face if he hadn't been the driver. "Wheels are hopelessly primitive. They require smooth-surfaced roads to travel on. Null-gravity can run over all surfaces."

That wasn't much of an answer, but, deciding not to expose any more ignorance, Jamie sat back and watched the parked spaceships and the looming city. Among the other transports gliding by were some that looked like glassed-in skateboards with seats. She figured it was a good thing they each didn't have one. Twenty-sixth-century London might not be ready for a wild young Viking on one of those.

But at the moment, Arni did not look very wild. He was sitting quite still, watching the strange sights, particularly the buildings.

These soared and arched and looped, like taffy stretched into odd shapes and then frozen. Surfaces gleamed with metallic harshness or with soft pastels. Nestled among these gravity-defying forms were older

buildings of stone and brick. They looked so familiar
and human, Jamie wanted to get out and hug them,
though she supposed the whole lot looked equally
strange to someone who'd grown up in a one-story
hovel with dirt and grass for a roof.

The people who walked or rode around the buildings, Jamie found equally astonishing. Many, she realized, must be full Kreeth. Their skin was green—not
Tyaak's muddy green, but a bright emerald. And their
hair, full-bristled or shaved in various styles, came in
every shade of blue from robin's egg to turquoise to
vibrant cobalt, though she saw none quite the inky
shade of their companion's. The Humans in the crowd
looked rather inconspicuous and colorless beside the
Kreeth.

There was also a sprinkling of different species.
Some had two arms, two legs, and one head. Some did
not. At the sight of these, Arni grabbed instinctively for
a dagger that wasn't there, then shrugged and just
stared.

The transport stopped, and Tyaak leaned back with
an exhausted sigh. "If I have not been acting on some
incredible delusion, the staff should be somewhere
around here."

They were in a plaza surrounded by three buildings.
One, of brick, was squat, with square towers and
peaked roofs. Another looked like a stretched wad of
pink bubble gum. The third, a metallic lavender, rose in
a more conventional rectangle except that its corners
were rounded and it pinched together in the middle. Its
sides seemed to be splattered with giant dribbles of glue
that might be sloping balconies. There were no obvious

windows on the latter two buildings, but clear patches seemed to be scattered over their surfaces like transparent fish scales.

"What do you say, Arni?" Tyaak asked.

The boy closed his eyes. "Up—way up. Old things about, and odd things, too. But many old things. At least they feel old from now."

"Old things," Jamie said. "That might be the brick place."

Arni looked at the five-story old Earth-style building. "No, a lot higher."

"Better see what the signs on the others say," Tyaak suggested. Stepping from the transport, he led them toward the bubble-gum building. Signs in several languages identified it as the Galactic Music Institute, Earth Subsection. The other, they saw when they walked to it, was the Institute of Earth Archaeology.

"Sounds more promising," Tyaak said, "if we are looking for old things."

Jamie nodded abstractly. "But what I'd really like to find is a restaurant. I'm starving."

"Me too," Arni added. "You do eat in this time, don't you?"

Tyaak laughed and walked toward the arched entrance of the lavender building. "There will be food dispensers in the lobby here. They are designed for a variety of species, so we should be able to find something for you."

The lobby was high and filled with free-form columns that looked to Jamie like wax dribbles on candles. She found the creatures walking between the columns even odder. Several Humans and a Kreeth were in a heated conversation with what looked like a rusty scrubbing pad. Something yellowish on tripod legs was walking between a Human and an almost transparent wormy creature. They approached what had to be an elevator. It opened and let out a Kreeth and a gray creature that reminded Jamie of the dancing hippos in *Fantasia*.

Scarcely noticing the building's occupants, Tyaak walked to a squat orange column, pressed some controls, and removed three long bars that shot into a tray. He handed Arni a gray one, gave a tan one to Jamie, and kept a black one for himself.

"Yours should taste like fish," he told Arni. "You do eat a lot of fish?"

"Not shaped like this." But the boy took a bite and then another. Jamie nibbled hers. It tasted nutty, and she decided not to ask for details.

Tyaak led them to the elevators. One slid open to let out two Humans. The three children stepped in and were joined by a female Kreeth whose hair seemed to fill up the remaining space. When she got out at one of the lower floors, the other three kept going up.

Tyaak had been riding with his eyes closed, but suddenly they popped open. "I think we just passed it." He touched the controls. Jamie couldn't sense any movement as she could in her time's elevators, but a light scale beside the door dropped again.

"No, passed it again," Tyaak said hitting the controls once more. "Here." The door slid silently open. They stepped into a wide space dotted with statues and display cases.

"What is this?" Jamie asked. "A museum?"

Tyaak shook his head. "Some of the lower floors are marked as museums." He pointed to a multilingual placard above what looked like a reception desk. "Archaeological Research Laboratory: Northern Europe."

"So, you think the staff's here?" Arni asked while peering into a case of squashed-looking reed baskets and sandals.

"What do you say?" Tyaak asked in return.

Arni frowned. "Not quite right. The height is, but there aren't enough old things around, or not the right old things."

Jamie could picture the staff now without even closing her eyes. She just willed herself to see it, and the picture snapped into focus in front of her. A moon-pale horse, carved as if leaping from the wood. It lay on blue-gray metal, shiny and cold. Dark green hands passed some instrument over it. A Human-looking pair of hands clamped wires onto the shaft. Then, briefly, another hand—a pale green hand pointing at something—fluttered into the picture.

Jamie blinked and looked at her companions. "There's a Human, a Kreeth, and that celery person doing things to it."

"Where?" Arni asked.

Jamie only shook her head, but Tyaak said, "Through there, I think." He nodded to a door beside the reception desk marked "Authorized Personnel Only."

"So, let's go," Arni said, heading for the door.

"No!" Jamie said. She realized suddenly that most eleventh-century Vikings couldn't read their own language, let alone the ones in which this sign was written.

"They'll stop us if we try to go in there."

The boy smiled. "Then we'll sneak by while they're looking at something else."

"What?"

"One of us could tip over that ugly statue. It should make a good crash."

"Yeah, and land one of us in jail, too," Jamie objected.

"Not if we do it from a distance," Tyaak said quietly.

Jamie shot him a questioning look.

"Well, this . . . this power, this thing you insist on calling magic, does seem to work."

Jamie frowned. "But everything we've been doing with it is sort of passive. Seeing or sensing things."

"What about what you and Arni did?"

"But that was using a staff," she said sharply. "We're on our own here."

Arni stopped staring at a pair of blue gangly people and joined the conversation. "Tyaak's right. If we are born sorcerers, we have magic *in* us. It's part of us. We should be able to make things happen with or without the staff."

Jamie felt cold inside. It had been the same all along. Arni was unafraid of magic because he totally believed in it, and Tyaak was unafraid because he believed that, if magic existed at all, it was just some other form of science. But she had only half believed. The half that still resisted, she admitted now, had glimpsed magic long ago and turned away in dread.

But the time had come to look again.

"Right," she forced herself to say. "Let's magic that great ugly statue right off its pedestal."

Chapter Fifteen

The three walked casually across the lounge, pretending to look at exhibits. A Human and a smaller version of the hippopotamus lady were examining something in one case. A gangly blue person, a Human, and a Kreeth with particularly spry hair were sitting around a table drinking coffee and discussing Bronze Age pottery.

Jamie joined the others by a case to the left of the reception desk and stared blankly at an exhibit about how to turn flint nodules into sharp tools. Inside, she was fighting with that old remembered fear. She had been a kid, sick in bed with the flu. She'd wanted a drink of water, but the glass was on a far table and she felt too weak to get up for it. So she lay there looking at the glass, wishing she could have it, pretending she could make it come to her. She'd imagined her hand closing around its smooth cool sides, imagined herself bringing it to the bed.

When the glass had actually come flying through the air, she'd been too startled, too terrified to catch it. It smacked into her pillow, splattering water all over. Her mother had been angry, and Jamie agreed that yes, she should have called someone instead of getting up herself. Then she buried the true memory as quickly as possible. There was no way that glass could have flown through the air on its own. If she had made that happen, she could do all sorts of things, frightening, unknowable things. It just hadn't happened. That recent moment in the Viking hall with the banner, had shaken loose the memory only a little.

But now it lay in front of her, a cold pool of fear she'd been trying to avoid for much of her life. And now she had to dive right into it.

At least she finally had an explanation—and a goal. And she was no longer alone. With the other two, she looked at the black metal sculpture across the room.

It would be cool to the touch, she was sure, but not smooth. The sculptor had pitted the surface with little pocks and bumps. Halfway up the twisted shape was a metal projection that hooked out like a misshapen cup handle. If she were to put a hand around that, she'd feel the cool rough metal against the palm of her hand, against the inside of her fingers as they wrapped around it. She would tighten her grip and feel the roughness press into her skin. She would tense her arm muscles and tug. Again, harder, and again. The sculpture would start to rock a little, then sway. Back and forth, back and forth until the piece was too off center. It would tip over. The sculpture's great weight would crash onto the floor, pointy parts gouging holes in the carpet.

A rending crash caught her attention. There was the sculpture, actually toppled over on the floor. She just stared. Tyaak grabbed her arm and pulled her after him. The reception people had rushed from behind the desk and didn't see three children slip through the forbidden door.

Beyond the door was a hallway with small rounded rooms on either side. Cautiously they followed the hall to a larger room, where boxes were stacked on tables, and other tables had objects spread over them. Jamie glanced around but didn't see the bone-white staff, and none of the tables was the right bluish gray. The others also shook their heads. They moved on.

Voices, arguing voices, were coming from the next room. Quietly, the three slipped to the doorway and listened.

"No, I don't see how we can allow that," a woman's voice said. "The technology by which it was found is unimportant. We are talking about a Human artifact over five thousand years old; it belongs here, pure and simple."

The answering voice was high and musical. Tyaak whispered that it must belong to the Valgrindol. "There is nothing pure and simple about this, and the technology does very much matter in this case."

A third voice chimed in, dry and rough, "The inspector is correct here. It was a routine energy survey that revealed the artifact, not an archaeological excavation."

"True," the Human voice admitted, "but it was

found in a major archaeological site that has never been thoroughly excavated, and it registers as contemporary with that site."

The lilting voice responded. "You forget, Director Johnston, that this is no ordinary Neolithic artifact we are discussing here. If it were, it would not be emitting the unidentified form of energy detected on the survey. It would not be defying all of our tests to determine the nature of that energy. If it were just a piece of five-thousand-year-old carved wood, we would gladly leave it on this planet for further study and display. But it is not."

Again the dry voice intervened. "Both of you have valid arguments, but really, Inspector, would it not be most appropriate for the initial study, at least, to be conducted here?"

"I am surprised at you, Commissioner. Surely as a Kreeth you do not have enough faith in Human technology to trust these people with such an important find."

"I object," Director Johnston interjected.

"As do I," the raspy Kreeth voice said. "In the years since contact, Human analytical technology has made considerable advances."

With a grunt the Valgrindol continued. "Since I outrank you both and hold a Beta security mandate, your objections are of little consequence. The object's archaeological importance is insignificant compared to what might be learned from studying the powerful energy it seems to be emitting. In light of the growing menace from those unexplained energy rifts in our neighboring sector, all new energy sources are of great security importance. So there must be no further delays.

I will leave with the artifact tonight and take it to the science station on Tarka Four."

The Human's voice was tight. "Very well. See to the artifact's packing yourself. I want nothing further to do with this."

At the sound of approaching footsteps, the three eavesdroppers crouched behind tables, but the woman stomping by was clearly too angry to notice much of anything.

Cautiously Jamie and the others stood and listened some more.

The trilling Valgrindol commented, "Your director certainly gets emotional, but that should be expected of Humans."

"It should be expected of any natives whose planet is losing control of an important artifact. I trust you will study it without destroying it."

"Yes, yes, Commissioner, of course. Now help me with the transport box. It's over there."

As the voices receded, the three children peered around the door. It was a large round room full of tables and odd-looking instruments. Its two occupants were walking to the far end. The Kreeth had sky-blue hair cut in a reverse mohawk, the sides bristly with a bare strip mown down the center. The Valgrindol was thin, totally hairless, and a pallid green. Jamie couldn't be certain if she was so repelled by the creature because it looked like a walking vegetable or because it might be one of the enemy, with its own reasons for wanting the staff. But other weird aliens hadn't made her skin crawl.

Without a word, she, Arni, and Tyaak crept into the

room to crouch beside a blue-gray table. The staff was lying there, exactly as Jamie had seen it.

Swiftly Tyaak reached out to grab it. But no sooner had his fingers touched the wood than the Valgrindol spun around. The face was as expressionless as a fish's, but the voice was not.

"So! I thought I felt some power here other than that staff. Let go of it!"

"No!" Tyaak yelled as he dashed for the door. He'd only gone a few steps before the Valgrindol snapped its fingers. A bolt of energy shot from its hand and wound like a fuzzy electrical snake around the staff. Tyaak struggled, but in a burst of sparks the staff was torn from him and whipped across the room.

"What was that?" the startled Kreeth demanded. "How did you—"

"Never mind. Catch those three! They are spies, saboteurs!"

But the three were already out the door. They ran through the other room, careened down the hall, and burst into the lobby. People—including the crew trying to raise the fallen sculpture—turned and stared.

"Not the elevator!" Tyaak called. "They could trap us there. This way!" He pelted down a side hallway, but Arni was soon out ahead. The red-haired boy reached a door, struggled with the unfamiliar handle, then flung it open.

"No, not that way!" Tyaak cried. "Over there!"

But it was too late. Several groups were already closing in, some with weapons drawn.

"On second thought . . ." Tyaak said, plunging out Arni's door with the others right behind.

As soon as she slammed the door behind her, Jamie knew this was a bad choice. Cold outside air. They were on a balcony, one of those they'd seen sloping down in short loops around the building. The air above was red with sunset—and the ground below was very far away.

Dizzily hugging the side of the building, Jamie shuffled after the others, trying not to look toward the uncomfortably low rampart. She picked up speed as she heard the door behind her open and close.

The sloping path rounded a corner and passed another door. Tyaak started to open it, but Arni had already run on. Shrugging, he hurried after the young Viking, with Jamie, feeling clammy and weak, sticking close behind. The path swung around another corner and dead-ended.

Arni squealed, skidding to a halt against the low wall. "Never mind," he said as the others nearly collided with him, "we'll use magic to turn invisible. If that doesn't work, maybe it'll help us fly."

Fly! Jamie thought as she slumped against the building's side. No way. Invisibility would work. She'd make it work! Imagine she wasn't here. She certainly didn't want to be. No one was here. Just empty air. Rough walls scoured by the wind. Empty space blowing with sunset light. Cold and empty nothing.

Footsteps and voices beyond the corner. A Kreeth peered around to their side, then turned back. "No, nothing there. They must have taken that other door. Go back."

Footsteps retreated; a distant door opened and closed. Silence. Jamie's trembling knees gave out and she sank to the narrow walkway, her feet braced against the low rampart, pushing her as far from the edge as possible.

No one said anything. The wind sang as it swirled around the odd shaped building. Far below in the distance, city gave way to shadow-smeared fields and darkened woods. Above, the sky flamed with red and purple, while along the horizon storm clouds piled into a dark wall.

Jamie shivered at the reminder. Storms. They had failed. The third staff would not be added to the other two. Urkar would fight his long battle alone. And he would lose.

"I always wanted to do something important," she said dully. "But I didn't expect to be the one who'd screw up and let the universe end."

Tyaak only nodded miserably, but Arni was looking thoughtful. "Tyaak, you mentioned 'energy rifts' and so did that grass-green guy. What are they? Are they part of Urkar's storm?"

"They are rips in the fabric of the universe, places where energy and matter get sucked in and vanish. But unlike black holes they spread, sometimes devouring whole suns. Usually they are isolated, but recently a number have been appearing and spreading in a nearby section of the galaxy."

Arni looked more confused than before, but asked no more questions. Tyaak ran his hand through his crest of hair, which was already beginning to go limp again. "It sounds crazy even to think of it, but energy rifts could be a manifestation of Urkar's storm. This 'magic' of yours may be just another way of seeing and working in the same universe. The forces Urkar talks about are very like the destructive forces of an energy rift or the creative ones at the heart of a star. Perhaps the only difference is whether you call the laws that govern them 'physics' or 'magic.' "

Jamie nodded. "And in either case, this chunk of the universe is gradually going to be destroyed, and those creepy folks working for the other side are going to be in the driver's seat until it is."

"Unless we can stop the storm," Tyaak said thoughtfully.

"But if we can't get hold of the third staff . . ." Jamie began.

Tyaak turned to her, looking grimly determined. "We have a goal. We failed to reach it one way, but there must be others."

"He's got a plan!" Arni crowed.

Tyaak laughed. "It hardly deserves such a grand name. It is more a chain of hunches. But first we must get back to the ship. They probably believe we have gotten away by now. Shall we try for real?"

He and Arni walked briskly up the sloping ledge to the nearest door. Eyes averted from the edge, Jamie crawled up after them.

They slipped through, and the door closed on the hollow emptiness outside, leaving them in an empty corridor. Jamie sagged against the solid wall, panting with relief. She couldn't deny that she had magic. She'd always sensed she could see ghosts, and that one terrifying try with the glass had made her refuse to admit she could move things without touching them. But Arni's suggestion of flying magically had never entered her wildest fantasies.

She didn't want to start with it now.

Chapter Sixteen

Tyaak found stairs; and for ages, it seemed, they spiraled down them, sharpening their ability to tell when someone was coming. When they couldn't dodge into hiding, they perfected the invisibility trick, thinking themselves into nothing but walls, floor, and empty space. Jamie was getting quite good at working with surface texture and angles of light.

Once outside, they ignored the transport they had come in, in case it was being watched, and walked several blocks to catch another back to the spaceport. It wasn't until they were locked in Tyaak's ship again that Jamie relaxed. She was surprised at that, considering how alien it was, but compared to twenty-sixth-century London, it felt like home. Arni, for whom this part of the adventure had seemed close to fantasy, was clearly less shaken.

"Got any more of those food sticks?" he asked. "That one was tasty but kind of small."

Tyaak went to a wall dispenser, produced several more and mechanically passed them around, his mind obviously elsewhere.

"So what's your plan?" Jamie asked as she bit gingerly into her pink food bar. "How are three kids going to snatch something that a bunch of scientists and a magic-working celery stalk are determined to take to another planet?"

"Well, that Valgrindol is one of the enemy all right, and it is aware of us. So it will be difficult to get to the staff while it is on Earth. But once they leave for Tarka Four, the staff will go into a cargo hold while the Valgrindol stays in the passenger section. That will be our chance."

Jamie looked skeptical. "But that ship's zooming off into space in a couple of hours. I'm sure Arni and I don't have the right credentials to buy tickets, and anyway, once we've got our stolen property, how do we get back with it?"

"Must you be so negative? We will not bother with tickets. When I was preparing to come to this planet, the ship's computers were loaded with all standard Earth transportation data: spaceport coordinates, arrival and departure routes, and so forth. It is not difficult to calculate the route for a ship departing this port for Tarka Four. We will simply leave now and intercept them on the way."

"Oh right, with all weapons blazing. Correct me if I'm wrong, but wouldn't your Valgrindol be traveling in a much larger ship with lots of firepower?"

"Certainly, but we will not be relying on firepower. We will use its opposite."

"How?"

Tyaak grinned. "What happened to your superstitious human 'belief' and 'trust'?"

"Oh, so it's 'Trust me,' is it?" Jamie shrugged and got up to see if she could work the food dispenser herself. "Well, I suppose we've been asked to do a lot crazier things lately."

Working the controls, Tyaak asked for and received permission from the spaceport to take off; speedily he did so. Jamie, not too pleased with the food bar she'd gotten, returned to her seat and the screen.

She watched London drop away beneath them, the older buildings lit at regularly spaced windows, the newer ones glowing all over like phosphorescent fungus. Then the city was just a patch of light in a dark island, an island surrounded by a darker sea, a sea spanning a dark planet.

Suddenly Jamie realized what she was seeing, and trembled as if she had a fever. That was her planet she was leaving, her home. All she had wanted was to be a little special, to do something her perfect brother couldn't—like maybe see ghosts. She hadn't wanted to go skipping through time, to have powers that terrified as much as they excited her. And she definitely hadn't wanted to leave her world on some space-piracy scheme that would probably mean she'd never see home again. She wondered if her ghost would end up haunting the spaceways some five hundred years after her time. At least if she met people who were looking for ghosts, she could warn them to forget the whole thing.

Jamie was just lying back, trying to relax, when the lights dimmed, the view screens went dead, and the slight trembling of the ship in motion slowed and stopped.

"What's the matter?" she asked in alarm.

Arni punched the lifeless viewscreen controls. "Did I break something?"

"No, I did," Tyaak replied. "At least I hope it will look like things are broken. The idea is to make this look like a ship in trouble. I have shut down all systems except for minimal life support; then I will damage some repairable reactor parts. When the Valgrindol's ship comes near, I will trigger a distress call. Space ethics require that the first ship in the vicinity of a vessel in distress stop and help. To save time, they will probably just bring us on board. Then we can steal the staff."

"Excellent!" Arni cried. "Those are Viking tactics!"

"Just back up a second," Jamie objected. "What if the first ship to come by isn't the right one?"

"It is almost sure to be. While still in a solar system, ships are required to keep strictly to regulation flight paths. Besides, we should be able to feel the staff when it comes close."

Jamie wasn't at all sure that would work in empty space but let it pass. What bothered her more was the next matter. "How do we get the staff once we're on the ship? They're not likely to give it to us as a souvenir."

Arni leaped up from his seat, waving his hand around as if it held a sword. "When Earl Thorfinn sailed away after the battle of Papey Stonsay, he had his men hide until the ship was in port. Then they jumped over the side and attacked Rogenvald's town!"

Tyaak smiled. "That is basically the idea. You two become invisible, and while I deal with the mechanic working on our ship, you find the staff and bring it back."

Jamie groaned. The number of things wrong with that plan was close to infinite. "But what if—"

"We will just have to do the best we can—unless you have a better idea, of course."

Sure. Thousands of miles out in space, in a twenty-sixth-century alien spaceship, where she couldn't even make the food dispenser work right. She shrugged. "No, go for it."

The cabin lights dimmed even further. "All right. No talking or noise now. I will set an alarm to alert us when a ship is approaching so I can trigger the distress call. Everyone just lie back and get some rest."

Rest, Jamie thought as she lay there tight as a spring. That word and "terror" just didn't go together. She looked over at Arni and was surprised to see him asleep already. Maybe Vikings were used to sleeping before battle.

On her other side, Tyaak seemed to be asleep as well. The bristles of his hair had calmed to a loose cascade. Suddenly she remembered where she'd seen hair that color before. Comic-book characters often had that same blue-black shade. For that matter, comics often did funky things with skin color too, though she hadn't seen them use much avocado green. Now, if only the outcome of all this were as safe and sure as in a comic book. Well, at least imagining the perfect happy ending would give her something to think about while the others slept. . . .

Jamie slept as well, a chime pulling her from a confusing cloud of dreams. Tyaak was already huddled over some controls, speaking weakly into a receiver.

". . . reactor nodes must have fused. All systems are down except for emergency life support, and that is going. I request immediate assistance. I repeat, anyone who can hear this: My primary reactor nodes must have fused. All systems . . ."

He repeated the message several times, throwing in sound effects by tapping his nails on the speaking grid. Jamie wanted to switch on her screen to see the approaching ship but knew the power was off. She wanted to stand up and pace, but had been told to keep down any noise the other ship's sensors might pick up. Arni was still asleep. Lucky kid.

Frustrated, she lay back and closed her eyes. Could she really tell if the staff were out there? She thought about the other staffs — the soaring black raven in Arni's world, the leaping golden fish in hers. She had felt their power, a warm tingling, a sense of . . . of what? Of something vast and mighty, just beyond what she could see and touch. Was she feeling a slight brush of that again? Or was it just a memory of the feeling?

In the darkness of her mind, she saw the staff again. Not as it had been, pale under a harsh light, exposed on a cold metal table. Here it was cocooned in fiber and nestled in close, confining darkness. The white arching horse glowed with a faint light of its own. Its warm power touched lightly at the familiar spot in her mind.

Her eyes flew open and she started to speak, but Tyaak shook his head, a hand to his mouth. Nodding,

she pointed in the direction from which she now knew
the ship was coming.

Quietly Jamie got up and tiptoed to Arni's seat, putting a hand over his mouth so he didn't make a noise
when she woke him. Then together they looked around
the cabin. With the lights this low, there were many
places where darkness could help even imperfect attempts at invisibility. They chose a spot on the far side
of the door and crouched down, trying to think about
being smooth metal walls and spongy beige floor. Nothing but air and wall and floor. Nothing at all.

Jamie was so into not being there that the sudden
clanking startled her. She forced herself to concentrate
again, ignoring the scraping sounds and the jarring
bump.

Tyaak had been fiddling with something behind one
of the wall panels — probably, Jamie realized, trying to
fake their technical failure. But now he sprawled himself over his seat like someone running out of air.

There was a tapping and scraping outside; then the
door opened. A Kreeth and a Human ran in, helped
Tyaak sit up, and gave him some sort of shot.

"Was such a fool," Tyaak gasped. "Thought this old
clunker was up to the trip. Didn't have a checkout
first."

Jamie didn't wait to hear this airhead Kreeth kid
bawled out. Still thinking about not being there, she
slipped out the open door, assuming Arni was behind
her. She couldn't see him. Reaching back, she flailed
around until she felt a hand and grabbed it.

She stopped short at the sight of two Kreeth examining Tyaak's ship, but they clearly didn't see her, so she

hurried on. They were apparently inside the rescuers' spaceship, in some large domed hangar. Several other ships larger than Tyaak's were sitting about on the wide metal floor.

When they were well away from anyone else, Jamie heard a voice whisper, "What do we do now? This keeping invisible is hard work."

She nodded, then realized he couldn't see that. "Agreed. But we'd better keep it up until we have the staff or at least until we're away from people. Any idea where it is?"

"Umm . . . crowded. A place like this, open, metal. But smaller and . . . crowded. Lots of things close up. Near the top, though."

A storeroom maybe, Jamie thought. She wished Tyaak were along; he was better at sensing directions. But he was busy giving her and Arni the time they needed, so they'd better not waste it.

"Well, let's start by going out that open door."

Still holding hands, they crossed a wide space where a gangly blue mechanic was working on a large dumbbell-shaped device. He didn't even look up. They slipped out the door; as soon as they reached the corridor, both turned left.

Yes, that felt right. The staff was this way somewhere.

"Up," a voice whispered behind her. "It's up from here."

There was an elevator, but they didn't know how to make it work. Not far beyond was a ladder. Jamie started up, saw feet coming down, and had to scramble back, nearly crushing her invisible companion.

Cautiously they started up again. The next floor was a slightly rounded corridor like the last. Arni had them go up more ladders, and more. He was right, she could feel it. They were getting closer.

Turning right, they hurried along another corridor until it intersected a second. For a moment they stopped; then Jamie felt Arni tug her to the left. Quickly she turned after him and ran smack into a Kreeth who had just stepped from a room.

Pain and surprise. Jamie lost concentration. The Kreeth gasped and stared. Jamie backed away, desperately thinking about corridors. Textured yellow walls. Two halves of a long tube cupping nothing but air between them. Empty air. Nothing else. Nothing there.

The Kreeth frowned and squinted. He took a step forward and patted the air in front of him. His spiky hair swayed as he shook his head, took a few steps farther, then abruptly turned and looked back. Still frowning, he walked away.

"Whew," Arni's voice said from nowhere. "This is wearing me out. But we're close, I think." A groping hand brushed against Jamie's and grabbed it again. She followed its tug down the corridor, being extra careful at each turn, until they reached a door. A closed, locked door.

"How do we get this open?" Jamie asked.

"You opened that door in the cathedral pretty well," came the reply.

"Yeah, but I had a staff then. And I kind of overdid it too."

Jamie put her hands against the door and felt Arni do the same. She felt like a safecracker, an incompetent one who didn't know how locks worked. Was this magnetic, electrical, or a combination lock? It would be better if there were no lock at all. Nothing to hold it. Nothing to keep the door from sliding open, sliding smoothly open as they pushed against it. Firmly pushing it sideways. Firmly sliding . . .

It opened. Jamie was sure that invisible Arni had the same astonished expression she felt on her own face. Quickly they stepped inside and slid the door closed behind them.

In yellowish half light, they could see a room about the size of a large garage. And it was full of stuff: crates and canisters, bales of things, tubes and boxes of all sizes. But at least they were the only people there.

Jamie leaned against a wall and let herself fade back into visibility. She felt as if she'd been holding her breath for a long time. Beside her, Arni appeared as well.

He sighed. "I'd never have guessed that not being somewhere could be so much work."

"The staff," Jamie said weakly. "You said it was near the top? It's in some sort of close-fitting container with fiber padding."

"This way, I think," Arni said, walking down an aisle between piled-up crates and canisters.

Jamie knew the box the moment she saw it. For a dizzy second she saw it from both inside and out. It was too high up for Arni to reach, but by stepping on a short, fat crate, she was able to wrap her fingers over the edge and tug the box off. Catching it, she was surprised at how light it was.

Arni fumbled at a clasp on the side. "Let's take the

staff and leave the box—then they won't see something's missing."

Jamie, too, fumbled at the clasp, then decided not to bother. Holding it, she imagined that it was the kind of clasp she knew: Lift here and it opened. It did open, though with a breaking sound that suggested her method wasn't quite what its manufacturers intended.

Inside, the long white staff glowed like captured moonlight through its nest of packing.

Jamie reached down and pulled it out. She smiled at Arni, then froze. Down the aisle of containers, she could see the door sliding open. Someone stepped into the room and looked right at them.

Someone tall, thin, and hairless, the exact color of celery.

Chapter Seventeen

"I knew there was power abroad other than my own," the voice trilled. "Ah, the two young Humans from the archaeological lab. On some sort of academic crusade, are we? Striving to keep Human archaeological treasures at home?"

"Yeah, that's right," Jamie said, knowing the lie was pointless even as she uttered it. "It belongs in a museum, not some analytical laboratory."

She couldn't tell about Valgrindol expressions, but the one she was seeing was surely a sneer. The creature stepped forward.

"You are right about it not really needing analysis. *We* know what its unidentified power is, don't we?" Swiftly the Valgrindol walked toward them down the aisle.

With a yelp, Arni hurled the long box at it and ducked around a corner. Stepping back, Jamie fell over the crate she'd used to climb on. Still sneering, the Valgrindol reached down.

Awkwardly clutching the staff, Jamie swiped it at the descending hand, crackling light through the air. Hissing, the creature drew back, then, spreading its hands, shot a tangle of light toward her. Jamie scrambled to her feet, only to have the light drop around her like a net. Desperately she hacked at the strands with the tip of the staff. They split and sizzled, freeing her to stumble back and around the corner. Arni grabbed her arm and pulled her down another aisle toward the storeroom door.

A sharp cracking sound made them look up. A tower of crates was shifting, falling toward them. Horrified, Jamie flung up her arm. The staff arched a shield of light raggedly above them. One crate hit the light and split open, sending a shower of round stones bouncing frantically over the floor.

Jamie and Arni scuttled forward, the shield collapsing behind them under an avalanche of crates and boxes.

Ahead of them, the Valgrindol had nearly reached the door. It pointed at another tower of crates and set it teetering. Jamie spun around and also pointed at it. The crates swayed back the other way. Then she felt another onslaught, and the crates tipped toward her again.

Out of the corner of her eye, Jamie could see Arni beside her. He reached down, scooped some of the round stones from the floor, and flung them at the Valgrindol. The handful he'd grabbed somehow swept the rest behind them, and a wave of stones rose from the floor and pelted their opponent. The creature's concentration was torn and the crates immediately fell toward it.

Jamie and Arni ducked out of the room, leaving the sounds of crashing and alien cursing behind them.

They charged down the corridor, with people turning and staring at them. "Go invisible!" Jamie shouted, struggling to make her mind do that as she ran. Empty air rushing along. Nothing in the corridor but air. It seemed to be working. One Human looked puzzled as something half seen rushed by, and the next group saw nothing at all.

Jamie stopped, confused, at one intersection, until Arni's voice led her down the righthand way. Suddenly the corridor lit up. A ball of sizzling light hurtled toward them. The Valgrindol inspector must have gotten out from under the boxes, Jamie thought as she stared terrified at the speeding light. Then, gripping the staff like a baseball bat, she swung.

The collision of energy flooded the corridor with sound and light. Using the smoking staff, Jamie pulled herself up from the floor. Dazed and visible, she could see all the scorch marks on her jumpsuit. She could feel them on her head and face.

Invisible hands hurried her down the corridor to a ladder. Awkwardly gripping the staff, she stumbled down. One flight, two, three. At the end she was sliding down the handrails rather than climbing.

Her head finally cleared from the light and noise. They must be on the right floor, because Arni was shoving her along the level now instead of down. She concentrated on being invisible again. People in the corridor listened in confusion to the sound of running feet.

"Stop them!" a high voice called from behind. "Two invisible thieves. There, on the left—block that corridor!" Clearly the trick didn't work on everyone.

A confused guard stepped into the middle of the passageway and held his arms out on both sides. Arni and Jamie ducked under and ran on. Feeling them pass, the guard swatted the air, but too late.

Suddenly on their right the wide door to the hangar appeared. An alerted guard stood nearby, weapon drawn, but they slipped around her and were through. Feet pounding invisibly over the metal deck, they dashed toward their little ship.

From nowhere a rope of cold flame snaked across Jamie's path, catching her around her knees and sending her sprawling facedown. The staff flew out of her hand, clattering and spinning across the deck.

Jamie lay stunned. Visibility crept back, and something heavy seemed to press her down. Beside her on the deck, Arni was lying flat as a lizard. A pinkish glow seemed to sit on them both. She couldn't even move her head. Skinny legs walked by, in the direction the staff had gone. A long pause; then the legs returned. They bent, and Jamie could see the celery-green face.

"I could turn you over as thieves to the security guards on this ship, but obviously you're too dangerous. So you'll simply have to disintegrate, spontaneously combust. I'll tell them you must have been on a suicide mission."

Jamie could see only the tip of the staff. If only she could touch it, feel it. But she could not. She'd never feel wood or anything from Earth again. She thought of the staff, of its smooth twisting grain and of the proudly lifelike horse carved on its top. Urkar had carved it, someone who clearly loved life, who loved his own harsh world and even his hapless descendants. But they had failed him and his world.

The light around them turned from pink to red to fiery orange. Mentally, Jamie tried to fight the heat, but still it grew, like the blast from an oven. Air was being sucked from her lungs.

Through the desert haze, she saw the Valgrindol moving away. Longingly she gazed at the staff, at the carved horse. Her last glimpse of home—of the staff's windy, cold, free home.

Her hair was beginning to singe and crackle. Over that sound she heard a sharp distant shout. Then a call, a wild animal call—like a horse's. Around her, the burning mist thinned, and the great weight lessened. She could move again. Half sitting, she stared. A great white horse was rearing up on the deck, bringing its hooves down again and again on a pale green form. Wind— cold, salty wind—swept through the hangar. For a moment, the metal deck seemed clothed with grass and purple heather. Sea foam broke on rocks, and birds screamed overhead.

Jamie and Arni struggled to their knees and then their feet. The image faded; a white wooden staff lay beside the fallen Valgrindol. The alien twitched feebly while yellow blood seeped over the deck. Around the hangar, people were yelling in confusion. Jamie stumbled toward the staff and grabbed it. She looked at their ship and saw Tyaak and the Kreeth mechanic standing in the doorway.

"What happened?" the mechanic called.

"Don't know," Arni yelled back. "But this fellow needs help." The Kreeth ran toward the injured Valgrindol as Jamie and Arni passed him, running for the ship. In moments, they were inside with the door closed.

Tyaak was squatting on the floor closing a panel in the wall. "There. Just had to snap in my hidden replacement." He stood up, then hurried to his seat and started working controls.

He flicked a brief glance toward them. "I was working with the mechanic, trying to keep him from seeing and solving the problem, when suddenly I felt a yearning, a longing for the island, for the windy cold place I loved—or that someone loved. The picture was so strong, I knew I had to call it back, to make it real."

"You did," Jamie said, "and it was beautiful."

Arni could only nod and add, "Thank you."

As their ship shuddered into life, Jamie asked, "Are they just going to open the door and let us go?"

"No. I think we will have to blast our way out of here."

"This little ship has weapons like that?"

"It does now." Grinning, Tyaak reached for the staff and, clutching it with one hand, began working a new set of controls with the other.

Jamie looked out her view screen. Humans, Kreeth, and others were pointing toward their ship. Suddenly they all began running away from it toward the hangar's inside door. She shifted the view in her screen. Something at the nose of their ship was glowing red.

A beam of light shot forward and beat against the outside door of the hangar. The metal paneling turned red, shifting to a blinding white. The door buckled and blew away, spinning out into star-filled space. In seconds, their ship shot after it.

"Will they chase after us?" Arni asked, focusing his screen on the large ship they were rapidly leaving behind.

"No. With all their important cargo and passengers, they will not throw off their schedule by chasing some minor thieves. But they are sure to report us to Earth Security, which will probably send a patrol ship out looking for us."

"That's not good," Jamie commented.

"No, it is not. They will be faster than we are. And better armed, conventionally at least. And I am not very sure how to work this staff yet, not for anything quick and accurate. I could end up hurting a lot of people I do not want to—including us."

Watching the stars out the view screen, Jamie was silent for a moment, then said: "Tyaak, even if we avoid patrols, won't you get in a lot of trouble? I mean, this is your time. It's not like my causing a ruckus in Viking times. That was centuries before my parents or passport officials were even born. But won't someone have recorded your ship's serial number or something?"

"Oh certainly, both on board the big ship and back at the spaceport. But I doubt it was the right number."

"Why?"

Tyaak smiled. "Making people see numbers that are not there is rather like making people not see things that are."

Jamie laughed. "See! Magic does have its uses."

He shrugged and turned away. "Not 'magic.' Just some science I do not quite understand yet. But until I do, there is no harm in making use of it."

Earth was again a large parti-colored ball on the view screens when they received their first security hail. Meekly Tyaak acknowledged and agreed to proceed to the London spaceport and give himself up.

"What," Arni protested, "give up without a fight?"

Tyaak grunted, adjusting some controls. "From here to London will take us along a northern trajectory. As we pass over the Orkneys, perhaps we can drop down before the security escort can stop us." He glanced at a screen to see a large well-armed security ship homing in on them. "And perhaps not."

The ship took up a position behind and above them, keeping at a steady, threatening distance. After a time Jamie ignored it and switched her screen elsewhere. They crossed from night to day and seemed to be coming in over the top of the globe. Great stretches of white showed below. "The North Pole!" She giggled. "Watch out for high-flying reindeer."

Both boys gave her completely blank stares. She shook her head. "Never mind. Just a dated folk belief."

Tyaak shrugged and turned back to his instruments. "Coming up on Orkney. I will take us in low. Suddenly dropping like a stone might give us a few seconds' advantage."

He stared at the view screen. "The clouds keep us from seeing the island, but I can feel it." On the screen, a swirling mass of cloud blanketed a portion of dark blue ocean. "Coming up, coming up. Now!"

Jamie, expecting the falling-elevator effect, felt nothing but a light dizziness. The main change came on the view screen. Clouds were coming up fast, a great roiling wall of clouds.

Tyaak ignored a beeping hail from the security ship and plunged on. Jamie swiveled her screen and saw the other ship streaking after them like a comet. Another ignored hail. Light shot from the pursuing ship and in moments exploded beside Tyaak's vessel, setting it rocking like a toy boat.

"A warning shot," Tyaak said.

"Here come the clouds!" Arni cried. "We can hide in them."

Tyaak shook his head. "They can track us by instruments."

"Ah," Arni said. "More magic."

"Sort of," Tyaak grunted.

The view screen showed billowing clouds, then went white as they plunged in. Worms of lightning seemed to burrow through the boiling mass. Abruptly the clouds parted, and black, storm-churned sea stretched beneath them. Tyaak jabbed a control, and the ship pulled up, skidding over the water just above the white caps.

"You needed to cut it quite that close?" Jamie squeaked.

"Almost. I was hoping they would either turn too late or lose confidence in flying by instruments and slow a little."

"Oh, and you wouldn't, I suppose?"

He looked at her sternly. "I can feel where I'm going, even if I can't see it."

She was about to jab back when light exploded jarringly beside them. Not lightning.

"Another warning shot," Tyaak said grimly. "Two is usually all the warning they give."

Above and behind them, the patrol ship shot out of the clouds, pulling up in time. It was closer than before and gaining. Ahead, a gray splotch spread over the dark sweep of ocean.

"They won't blow us up, will they?" Jamie asked. "Surely stealing an old stick isn't a capital offense."

"Perhaps not. But resisting arrest makes police types awfully mad."

Suddenly their little ship bucked and lurched. The view seemed washed with yellow.

"No!" Tyaak yelled in frustration. "A capture beam. We must be just within range." He pointed angrily at the view screen. "And look, we are so close! We are almost home!"

They slowed. The wave-battered coastline inched closer and passed beneath them. Below spread grassy moors splotched with heather. Hills and lochs marked the distance but drew no nearer. They were stopped dead, a few miles from their goal.

Chapter Eighteen

Tyaak's dark face took on a look of stubborn fury. "We cannot let them stop us now!" He jumped up and grabbed the wooden staff. "Our engines need more power, and even if the strain tears this ship apart, they will have it!"

He splayed one hand over the engine controls and with the other clutched the staff. Beside him, Arni and Jamie exchanged the same look of stubborn conviction. Each wrapped a hand around the staff and placed another hand on Tyaak's.

Jamie felt like a tiny electrical component connecting two massive forces. Part of her stretched out, vibrating in tune with the engine's straining, rumbling strength. The other part reached into a deep vent of tingling power that welled up and burst through her.

The ship jerked forward, metal screaming, engine whining. Slowly the landscape began moving again.

Jamie's every fiber felt stretched and frayed like a rope in tug-of-war. Ahead, two lochs glinted silver under the stormy sky. They dragged farther and farther forward. So very slow, Jamie thought. Could they possibly make it before the ship blew apart? She strained her eyes and thought she could make out a faint circular mark beyond where the two lochs met, a tiny scattering of gray stones.

One loch passed beneath them, its slate surface churned by the wind. Ahead of them lay the circle; but around them, the ship howled like a dying wolf. Closer, slowly closer. Almost beneath them. They were directly overhead.

The change was so sudden, they all staggered and nearly lost their footing. Below, the circle was perfect again, every stone whole and upright. Jamie scanned with her view screen, but the other ship was gone — or rather, she guessed, *they* had gone, leaving a perplexed police crew alone over a nearly deserted island.

But here no longer seemed an island of eternal stars and stillness. Their ship rocked and plunged as if heaved about by a storm. Above, the stars were blotted out by roiling black clouds fringed with lightning.

Fighting the controls, Tyaak brought the ship spiraling down to a rough landing within the circle. It was difficult even opening the door against the wind, but finally they forced it back, letting in a blast of cold and wet. Struggling for every step, they crawled out, Tyaak clutching the staff. The wind howled like a vengeful beast.

As if with a swipe of its paw, it knocked Jamie from her feet. It tumbled and tossed her like a leaf across the heather, until she smacked up against a standing stone. Even the stone seemed to tremble from the wind and the constant bombardment of thunder.

Lightning lit the rain-lashed circle in irregular flashes. Jamie strained to see the center. A lone man stood there, clinging to a pillar, a pillar made of two entwining staffs. The boys were slowly fighting their way to him.

Jamie shoved off from the stone and, digging her fingers into the heather, she slowly pulled herself forward. Over the thunder, wind, and pummeling rain, she heard words, snatches of song. The lone figure in the center was hoarsely chanting into the sky; the twined pole he clung to glowed faintly.

She was closer now, and so were the others. Pulling himself with one hand, Tyaak stretched the staff forward. Urkar stretched his free hand toward it. With a final strain, he grasped the staff and pulled it in.

Staggering, the man raised his voice above the storm and jabbed the point of the staff into the earth beside the other two. From where they touched, a glow spread upward and the staffs twisted and coiled together, growing like living things. The carved beasts pranced and flew and dove around one another until they became one creature with wings and fins and flashing hooves. Its cry split the air.

The three children reached the pillar's base and pulled themselves upright. Under their hands, they felt the wood's vibrant warmth as energy passed from them and to them. The glow stretched across the ground in spokes of light reaching toward the stones. With the touch of that light, each trembling stone steadied and itself began to glow. The glow strengthened to a white glare, becoming stronger and stronger until the stones could no longer contain it. Light shot from the top of each, powerful white beams piercing the storm-blackened universe.

The circle of light beamed upward, blending into a single shining column, its core glowing and pulsing with life. Urkar and his descendants clutched the core and each other, feeling life run through them to the sky, an unending single force.

It all may have lasted forever or only for seconds; when Jamie was next aware of time, the great pillar she had seen around her was etched in only the faintest trace of light. The sky above was black and infinite, set with crystal stars. The sound of the storm was distant, fading into utter quiet.

"Well," Urkar said into the trembling silence, "I suppose that waiting for a brood of stubborn, goal-oriented relatives was worth it after all."

They didn't need a campfire now. As they sat around it in the heather, light and healing warmth came from the entwined wooden core. "I've got to admit," Urkar said, running a hand through his mop of forever graying hair, "you three had much more power than I ever guessed."

"Or than I guessed," Arni said, unconsciously copying the gesture with his own red hair. "It's so different from being good with the sword. I suppose I'll have to be a little careful how I show power or use it."

"And so will you all," Urkar cautioned. "Each one

of you comes from a time when this power is neither understood nor trusted—except, of course, by those who share it on one side or the other. You'll have to teach yourselves and take care how you practice. There's a great deal more to it than you've yet guessed. Magic is a difficult heritage."

Tyaak shook his mane of flowing hair. "There is certainly more to my heritage than I ever expected." He laughed. "Perhaps I will continue wearing my hair like this."

Jamie grinned at him. "An outstanding idea."

Arni looked at Urkar. "But if there's so much we have to learn, why can't we stay here a while and have you teach us?"

"Me? A teacher? Preposterous! I haven't the patience."

Jamie gave an indignant snort. "Urkar, that's just a line, and you know it. You waited around here for centuries and centuries."

"Yes, but not patiently."

Tyaak laughed. "Stubborn, isn't he? But what are you going to do now that the waiting is over?"

"Oh, but it isn't. That's the rub. Eternity is a long time, and that storm will always be out there ready to break." He looked around at the three young faces. "It's the same in any individual life, the constant struggle between creation and destruction. But you, at least, will be aware of it, and you will not be alone. There will be others who are with you, whether they know it or not." The man smiled wryly. "And I guess I won't be quite as alone either. If I need help again, I'll know where to find it."

"We'll be ready!" Arni said, jumping up and waving his sword arm in the air.

Urkar chuckled. "Well, you're not ready to go home like this—soaked, cold, exhausted. Come, one last time, sleep within the circle."

The wind was sharp and tinged with rain, but it didn't chill her as much as did the feeling of loss. Jamie sat up and looked around. The stones were tilted and only half were standing. Beyond them the moors were marked by fields, roads, and the occasional house. The wind froze the tears on her cheeks. She was home, and she had never felt so alone.

Arni and Tyaak had been like brothers, bothersome and precious at the same time. And now she'd never know the rest of their stories. One had already been told and forgotten, and the other had not yet been written. How had it been for Arni when he returned? Did he become what he wanted to be? And Tyaak, would he find a place for himself in that strange universe of his?

She'd never know; yet, oddly, she was sure that things were or would be right with both of them. Somehow, she still felt a part of each, as they would always be a part of her.

Jamie looked about the bleak landscape. No, not so bleak. It had its beauties. And it was part of her too.

The rain had stopped. It took a moment to recall where she had last left this time. Yes, the people from the cathedral. Some present-world time seemed to have passed, in which they'd given up and gone back. She'd have to hurry to get to the house before her parents.

Maybe she'd even suggest going bird-watching with them tomorrow. She'd kind of like to see more of the island, Jamie thought, admitting with a smile that it did get into a person's blood after a while. But wait, she remembered queasily, weren't they planning on taking a boat to one of those other islands? Another stomach-turning boat trip.

Running her hand through her hair, Jamie laughed. Then, stretching out her arms, she spun around happily in the heather.

Yes, she would have to be patient with this magic thing. She'd have to teach herself carefully how to use it and always be on the lookout for threats from the other side. And, too, she'd have to not let herself get too splashy trying to show that Jamie Halcro could be better at something than her brother. But still, she ought to at least be able to use magic to keep her from getting seasick!

With a jaunty wave at a passing blue-eyed seagull, Jamie marched out of the circle, boldly ignoring the signs about keeping to the path.